A Selborne Year

Gilbert White

A Selborne Year

The 'Naturalist's Journal' for 1784

Edited by   Illustrated by
Edward Dadswell · Nichola Armstrong

Webb & Bower
MICHAEL JOSEPH

First published in Great Britain 1986 by
Webb & Bower (Publishers) Limited
9 Colleton Crescent, Exeter, Devon EX2 4BY

in association with
Michael Joseph Limited
27 Wright's Lane, London W8 5SL

Designed by Peter Wrigley
Production by Nick Facer

British Library Cataloguing in Publication Data

White, Gilbert
A Selborne year: the naturalist's journal
for 1784.
1. Natural history—England—Selborne
(Hampshire)
I. Title   II. Dadswell, Edward
508.422′74   QH138.S4

ISBN 0–86350–098–6

Typeset in Great Britain by
Keyspools Ltd., Golborne, Warrington, Lancashire
Printed and bound in Italy by
New Interlitho SpA

Gilbert White and the Naturalist's Journal

Gilbert White was born at Selborne, in 'the extreme eastern corner of the county of Hampshire', in 1720. For technical reasons he could never be vicar of Selborne, but his native place meant more to him than thoughts of a 'fat goose living', as his friend John Mulso says, and he settled there permanently in the mid-1750s. He had already taken charge of the garden at The Wakes, the house in the centre of the village, and in 1751 he had started to keep diary/notebooks. His *Garden Calendar* covers the years 1751 to 1767, and he made a 'calendar of flora', a one-year survey of the wild flowers of the parish, during 1766. The *Naturalist's Journal* is the third and longest of his diaries: it was kept almost without a break from 1768 until the time of his death, at seventy-three, in June 1793.

The *Naturalist's Journal* was a source White used regularly in working on the letters and papers which eventually made up *The Natural History of Selborne*, the only work he published. (The description of the 'lop and top riot' in the 1784 *Journal*, for example, was incorporated into *Selborne* virtually unchanged.) But the *Journal* is both a record of work in progress and a portrait of the parish in its own right. A seasonal account in annual volumes, it includes not only 'natural history' but gardening and farming notes; and it shows us the domestic and sociable White, as he bottles his wine or makes jam, or interests himself sympathetically in the lives of his neighbours. Each year of the *Journal* was based on a printed *pro forma*, the 'invention' of Daines Barrington, the second of the two naturalists to whom the *Selborne* letters are addressed, although plain pages could be added to the printed pages. The format was particularly suited to someone who kept records meticulously and was a master of apt, concise description. White refused to be hurried into print, and *The Natural History of Selborne* did not appear until the winter of 1788–89; but in addition to keeping his journals—and a 'chronicle' of the regular beer and wine-making undertaken at The Wakes, and his account books—he was a busy letter writer and an occasional poet. Considered from one standpoint, the *Journal* is itself a sort of poem. 'Goose sits; while the Gander with vast assiduity keeps guard; & takes the fiercest sow by the ear & leads her away crying', he writes in March 1769. Tiny and 'abject' creatures received his special attention, and in December 1789 he described the behaviour of a house-fly:

> 'A *musca domestica*, by the warmth of my parlour has lengthened out his life, & existence to this time: he usually basks on the jams of the chimney within the influence of the fire after dinner, & settles on the table, where he sips the wine & tastes the sugar & baked apples. If there comes a very severe day, he withdraws & is not seen.'

But the entries—however they are considered—belong in a context, in any instance; and the *Journal* is seasonal but by no means merely repetitive. The 'portrait' can vary greatly from one year to another. The weather of the Selborne locality is capricious, and during the second half of the eighteenth century was often more extreme, in summer or winter, than is usual in southern England today. And the 'years' vary too depending on White's own preoccupations. The 1781 *Journal* is dominated by the effects on the parish of the drought which continued for much of that year; and the 1777 *Journal*, while illustrating his long-term pursuit of various natural history questions, and reflecting seasonal changes, tells the story of the building of the 'great parlour', the room he added to the Selborne house, though not without some emergencies and interruptions.

Weather crucially shapes each of the *Journal* years, however. (Rain was the chief interrupter of work on the great parlour.) White was a pioneer student of what he called the 'life and conversation' of animals and plants; he was concerned with the first-hand observation of the behaviour of living things, where other naturalists of his time were more likely to make collections of (usually dead) specimens. He considered most of his living creatures over periods of many years and in their ecological settings, moreover. Social relations were important in much animal and even plant behaviour, he saw, and so were food supplies and cover, and therefore also soils and climate. In the *Journal*, human activities are far more prominent than in *Selborne* itself, but men and women too live in environments (they are or can be viewed as part of 'natural history', by Gilbert White). By comparison with an urban population or a later age, the human members of the Selborne parish were particularly vulnerable to seasonal conditions; for one thing, they were most of them involved to some extent in agriculture. Of necessity, therefore, they treated the weather with the greatest respect, a respect constantly echoed in White's writings.

1784, as White describes it, took its character largely from sudden weather changes. There were oddities of weather, such as the freak hailstorm which occurred in June; it struck only part of the parish, but it had lasting effects on some of the growing crops. The year was to be eventful in other respects too—although no indication of this could have been gathered from its first quiet and 'backward' months.

White was in his sixty-fourth year but made one of his periodic visits to South Lambeth early in 1784. He was the eldest of five brothers who lived on into adulthood, and on these visits he stayed with either Thomas or Benjamin White, one a merchant and the other a bookseller and publisher. At South Lambeth, then still a village, he was within easy reach of London, and it was during one of these visits, in 1767, that he first met Thomas Pennant, the other naturalist he is 'writing to' in *Selborne*. Returning on April 1st, he found the parish still partly covered in snow; the winter had dragged on at Selborne, which no doubt explains the 'rioting' over lop and top firewood which had taken place in the Holt forest.

The late spring retarded the plant life, and he notes the greatly reduced numbers of blackbirds and thrushes, and the non-appearance of the ringouzels which usually passed through his region in April. The tortoise did not emerge until April 23rd, where in a warm spring he was sometimes out by the beginning of the month; and he saw his first bats of the year only on April 29th.

The first of the abrupt changes which were to typify the year took place at the beginning of May; warm 'summer weather' was recorded, and on May 16th 'sultry heat'. Writing to his niece Mary, or Molly, the daughter of Thomas White, he tells her, 'We have leaped this year from winter to summer at once, like the countries round the Baltic . . . the Tulips, as soon as blown, gape for breath and fade.' An idyllic late spring period followed, lasting from mid-May until the beginning of June, and the great hail-storm occurred on June 5th. The summer was cool and often wet, though it too was variable. He ricked his hay early in July in 'delicate order', and on August 16th was referring in a letter to 'sweet harvest weather', but rain repeatedly held up the harvesting, and late in August we hear of wheat lying in a 'sad, wet state'. (At the end of the year he gives monthly rainfall tables for Selborne, Fyfield near Andover, the home of his brother Henry, and South Lambeth. All had relatively wet summers in 1784, we find, but the summer rainfall at Selborne was by far the greatest.)

The naturalist/curate identified with his village, and his anxiety during these weeks is plain, but much of the wheat was saved; with another turnabout, September was hot and dry for the most part, and October was dry, calm and warm. The hop-pickers now earned good wages, and with his helpers White gathered huge crops of apples and 'Swan's egg, autumn-burgamot, Cresan-burgamot, Chaumontelle, & Virgoleuse pears'. Apricots were plentiful at The Wakes, and were boiled and bottled, and his nectarines and peaches ripened well.

On October 25th, keeping up the sequence of sudden changes, and heralding the end of the 'golden weather', there was a sharp frost and a snow shower. The foliage began to turn strangely dusky, and the beech hanger was almost leafless by November 8th. There were no acorns at Selborne in 1784 (by contrast with 1783, when the crop was 'prodigeous', following a hot, dry summer), and there was little beech mast. Both were of interest to an 'outdoor naturalist', and in a village where most householders kept a pig, both were of practical importance. The whitethorns, however, were loaded with haws. They must have benefited the blackbirds and thrushes, and their 'congeners' the newly arrived fieldfares, for during the second week in December a period of intense cold set in. Snow began to fall heavily on December 7th, and it continued all the next day and night; as the scene is described in *Selborne*, 'the works of men were quite overwhelmed, the lanes filled so as to be impassable, and the ground covered twelve or fifteen inches without any drifting.' (*Selborne*, DB lxiii) Sheep were buried in the snow, and the lowest temperature White ever recorded—thirty-three degees below freezing on the Fahrenheit scale—occurred on December 10th. Deep snow remained

until the end of the year, although a thaw was beginning during the final days of the year.

The great hail-storm of 1784 is also described in *Selborne* (DB lxvi); but his close observation of its consequences later in the year—for instance, its unexpectedly beneficial effect on some of the hop gardens—is not referred to there. He did not think of the *Selborne* 'letters' as a vehicle for farming observations, and similarly the detailed gardening records he kept annually were not made use of extensively in the work he published. His knowledge of farming and, most importantly, his achievement as a gardener have sometimes been underestimated as a result. He had largely created the beds and walks, the orchard and extensive vegetable garden he gave so much attention to, and as he left them his garden and smallholding covered some eleven acres: the 1784 *Journal* indicates, at least, the great range of his gardening activities. Gardening was one of his greatest pleasures, but gardening and farming were part also of a constant practical economy. He had inherited his house but very little money came to him from his parents. His soil at The Wakes was a hard gardening soil, a stiff chalk marl, which required constant 'amelioration' to render it workable. (In February 1784 we find him broadcasting large quantities of peat ashes on one of his fields.) But he tackled it with his usual busy determination.

Balloons and ballooning are not referred to in *Selborne*, but they were a major feature of the later summer and autumn of 1784. In the outside world the year was one of balloon excitement, as had been the historic 1783, and Selborne was not to be left out. The warm, clear autumn weather was particularly appropriate (ballooning too takes place in an environment), and White's nephew Edmund was trying out a model hot-air balloon at Newton Valence, on the other side of Selborne Down, on September 3rd. On September 24th Gilbert was writing to Mary White, 'O Molly! you don't tell us of the balloon, and the ascent of Mr. Lunardi: did it not affect you, to see a poor human creature entering upon so strange and hazardous an exploit', and he goes on, 'I wish the newspapers would learn to talk with a little more precision about thermometers. In the late accounts they represent Mr L and his apparatus covered with ice at 35°, three degrees above the freezing point.' When a balloon and balloonist, this time Mr Blanchard, was due to pass over Hampshire, on October 16th, he realized it would be visible from Selborne—and he rose to the occasion. He studied the prevailing wind, and worked out (correctly) the time when the balloon could be expected. He alerted all his neighbours and wrote to 'Farmer Pink of Faringdon', who, we know, took it as idiosyncrasy and was chastened when the wonderful event took place. Though his heart bounded with joy and fear, Gilbert himself

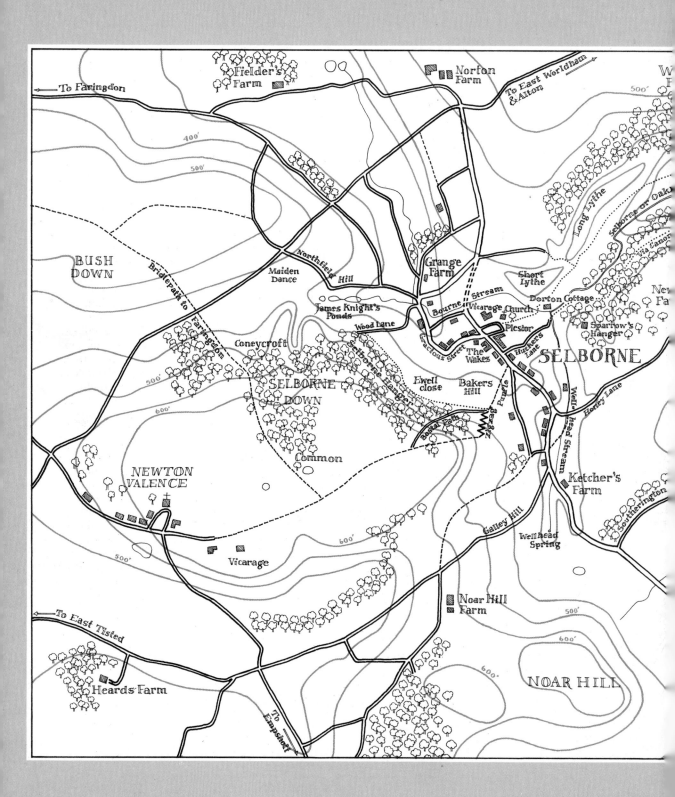

'The high part to the south-west consists of a vast hill of chalk ... At the foot of this hill, one stage or step from the uplands, lies the village, which consists of one single straggling street, three quarters of a mile in length, in a sheltered vale, and running parallel to The Hanger.'
(*Selborne*, TPi)

Two streams rise on the lower slopes of Noar Hill, White points out. One becomes the Selborne or Oakhanger stream and eventually joins the River Wey, and the other becomes the Rother—the shorter of the two Sussex Rothers—and eventually joins the Arun.

observed the balloon through a telescope, and then, as we would expect, made detailed, accurate notes. In the following January he recorded the crossing of the Channel by Blanchard and Jeffries; in his words, 'These are the first aeronauts that have dared to take a flight over the sea!!!'

Other members of the Selborne community appear repeatedly in the 1784 *Journal*. Goody Hampton was White's summer 'weeding woman'; she was a hard worker and 'excepting that she wears petticoats, and now and then has a child, you would think her a man'. Thomas Hoar was his trusted general assistant; he had been taught to read and write by Gilbert, and could not only be left in charge of the garden but could take daily meteorological readings when his master was away. 'Butler' was a thatcher, and Timothy Turner a neighbour and smallholder, and there are references to various of the village shopkeepers (for instance, John Burbey the grocer, whose pet owl White was to immortalise), and parish farmers, some of whom were longstanding friends and with all of whom he could exchange country information and local news. The effects of climate he drew attention to were often effects on people, I said. The community as a whole would have suffered had the wet harvest weather continued in the late summer of 1784, for not only were the 'poor' employed in large numbers by the farmers but many of the village residents grew wheat or barley as 'copyholders', and 'every decent labourer also has his garden'. He himself repeatedly displayed the skills required to live in the Hampshire village. He records in mid-September that 'the heats are so great, & the nights so sultry, that we spoil joints of meat, in spite of all the care that can be taken'. But he gardened, on a greater or smaller scale, the whole year round; and in December 1784, as the temperature fell sharply, he was successful in the measures he took to protect his foodstuffs from the frost.

The meandering lanes made access to the parish difficult even in the summer months, but as visiting friends and relatives come and go during 1784 we realize that White, though he was without co-workers of his own insight and ability, was not the solitary figure tradition has sometimes made him. Molly, the favourite niece, who sometimes did copying and research work for him, did not arrive until late in the autumn, but John Mulso visited him with his family in July. He and White had been friends since their college days, and the good-natured Mulso, always in more comfortable circumstances than Gilbert himself, took a genuine interest in his welfare. Brother Henry (or Harry), his wife and two of their children stayed at The Wakes briefly during the summer, and a ship's officer who was visiting the village in June and July spent time also with Gilbert White. Brother Benjamin—the publisher of natural history books, including in due course *The Natural History of Selborne*—was at

Newton Valence for part of the summer, and Thomas White was at The Wakes throughout December. (Molly had returned to South Lambeth without him, we know, and he had been caught at Selborne by the heavy snow.) Gilbert, a batchelor, though by now with the widow of his brother John as housekeeper, kept a careful tally of his nephews and nieces, and in October 1784 he recorded the birth of the 41st of these. His affection for children is obvious from many of his notes, and while he welcomed all his visitors, the younger ones were those perhaps with whom he was most at ease.

His parish, White tells us in *Selborne*, 'is full of hills and woods, and therefore full of birds'. Inevitably, wild fauna and flora are a staple interest in the *Naturalist's Journal*, even if they there take their places with the other Selborne inhabitants and visitors. In 1784, a wood pigeon nests in his American juniper, bearing out his observation that wood pigeons and missel thrushes, both of them species which are otherwise shy and wary, will often make use of gardens and orchards at nesting time. And early in the year he gathers some more data of relevance to whether any of the 'swallow kind' hibernate during the winter. The hibernation/ migration controversy was still unresolved in his day, and as with various of his other enquiries, his interest in this 'puzzle' continued throughout the period covered by the *Journal*, or until the time of its abrupt discontinuation. Again, the reader who is himself a bird watcher will notice the reference to 'uncrested wrens', White's collective name for the three leaf warblers—the chiff-chaff, the willow warbler and the wood warbler; he was the first to distinguish these three species authoritatively, but even he, the master observer, could not tell them apart easily when they were not in song. A large flock of ravens would assemble over the Selborne beech hanger, we find, where today the raven is virtually unknown in Hampshire. (In White's time there were still great bustards in Sussex and Hampshire, and he saw some himself on Salisbury Plain.) Even without leaving his own grounds, he could enjoy a profusion of birds

The rain in August was ___ 3 = 88. — [inch: h.]

My Nep: Edm.d White & Mr Clement launched a balloon on our down, made of soft, thin paper; & measuring about two feet & an half in length, & 20 inches in diameter. The bigest air was supplyed at bottom by a plug of wood with spirits of wine, & set on fire by a candle. The air being cold & moist this machine did not succeed well abroad: but in Mr Yalden's stair-case it rose to the ceiling, & remained suspended as long as the spirits continued & flame, & then sunk gradualy. These Gent: made the balloon themselves. This small exhibition explained the whole affair very well: but the position of the flame wanted better regulation; because the least vacillation set the paper on fire.

A Faringdon man shot a young fern-owl in his orchard.

Wheat carted all day.
Swallows gather on the tower.
Many pease abroad, that have lain for weeks.

Farmer Town began to pick his hops: the hops are many, but small. They were not smitten the hail, grew at the S.E: end of the village. Hopping begins at Hartley.
The two hop-gardens, belonging to Farmer Spencer & John Hale, that were so much injured, as it was supposed, by the hail-storm on June 5th shew a prodigious crop, & larger & fairer hops than any in the parish. The owners seem now to be convinced that the hail, by beating off the tops the buds, has encreased the side-shoots, & improved the crop. Que: therefore, should the tops of hops be pinched-off when the be... (are very gross, & stro...

The *Naturalist's Journal* for 1784, Aug. 29th–Sept. 4th,
left-hand page.

THE NATURALIST'S JOURNAL. 41

Year Place. Soil.	Therm.	Barom.	Wind.	Inches of Rain or Sn. Size of Hail-st.	Weather.	Trees first in leaf. —Fungi first appear.	Plants first in flower: Mosses vegetate.	Birds and Insects first appear, or disappear.	Observations with regard to fish, and other animals.	Miscellaneous Observations, and Memorandums.
Silborne. Sunday. 8 Aug. 29. 12 4 8	60.	29 4·10	SW.		sun & clouds. pleasant sprinkling. gloomy dewy.			Much wheat abroad. Much tremella on the grounds.		
Monday. 30. 8 12 4 Full moon. 8	55. 60.	29 4·10	NE. SE.		hoar dew. sun & clouds. dark. rain.		Peaches & nectarines swell & grow; but want warm, dry weather to ripen them, & give them flavour. Grapes are very backward.			
Tuesday. 31. 8 12 4 8	60.	29 3·10	SW. S.	15.	rain, rain. sun & clouds. sun, fine afternoon.			Fly-catchers still. No wheat housed. Heavy clouds in the horizon.		
Wednes. 8 Sept. 1. 12 4 8	60.	29 6·10	NE. SE.		deep fog. gleams of sun. dark milky & still.			Swallows gather on the tower. Wheat housed.		
Thurs. 2. 8 12 4 8	57½ 64.	29 8·10	NW. S.		grey, mild. sun & clouds. fine harvest weather, gale.		Timothy comes forth into walks. The weather has been so cold that it has not been out for some time. Much wheat housed. Harvest moon.			
Friday. 3. 8 12 4 8	59. 63.	29 9·10 29 9·10	SE. S.		grey. mild. sun. hot sun. sweet even.		China-asters begin to blow. Saw a white-throat in the (garden.) Sweet harvest weather. Wheat ricked, & housed. Mich: daisies begin to open. N°. Many uncrested wrens			
Saturday. 8 4. 12 4 8	58½ 68.	29 9·10 29 8·10	SE.	fog	vast dew. sun, cloudless. golden weather. red even:		still appear. Wheat will be finished off to day pretty well. Fly-catchers seem to be withdrawn. Swallows cluster on the cherry-trees at the parsonage. Tyed up more endive: endive very large. Ant-flies swarm. The scars, & wounds on the birds, made by the great hailstones, are still very visible.			

...find this practice to be of great ...vice with melons, & cucumbers.

we may well envy him today. Towards the end of May 1784, the nightingale, nightjar, cuckoo and grasshopper warbler could all be heard at the same time in the evening in and from his 'outlet', the garden and meadow below his terrace.

His gentleness stopped well short of sentimentality, it is clear. His interest in the behaviour and 'conversation' of other creatures set him apart from those in the village for whom to find something rare or unfamiliar was as a matter of course to try to catch or shoot it, but when two tortoises which had been brought down to  Selborne by coach died, in July 1784, apparently from injuries received on their journey, he immediately cleared and examined 'the contents of their bodies'. In another age he might have added writing for children to his many other activities, and he did write the *Letter from Timothy the Tortoise to Miss Hecky Mulso*; but, perhaps to the surprise of some Selborne enthusiasts, he approved the killing of the hares which invaded the village gardens during periods of hard frost. He was not a visitor to Selborne, we have to remember.

1784 was a representative Selborne year, even allowing for Blanchard's balloon. White, a many-sided man and naturalist, was a champion of 'Selbornian scenes', but willingly kept up his contacts with the outside world. He was a scientific naturalist, by intention, if he was also an essayist and poet, and although he was never a fellow of the Royal Society, his papers on the 'hirundines' were published in the *Philosophical Transactions*. His district provided him with widely diversified conditions in which to observe and study, and making use of this diversity, he could probe and investigate his parish creatures, as well as describe and celebrate them. A nesting style may seem to be instinctive, and yet may be suited to local and peculiar conditions, as with the 'suburban chaffinches and wrens' he describes in *Selborne*. But, as the *Journal* in particular shows, White was himself diversified. He had been born at Selborne, and yet his parish constantly surprised him; 'You are more able to see with your own eyes, than any man I know', John Mulso told him. He was unassuming—the pride he took in his local 'mountains' and 'forests', or in his own cucumbers or wall fruit, illustrates this unassuming character; the large 'statue of Hercules' he erected on the far side of his garden had been made for him by John Carpenter the village carpenter—and yet a genius for intimacy, as it has been called, informed his social relations and his work as a naturalist and gardener. He died at Selborne on June 26th, 1793. On June 13th he was writing in the *Journal*, 'Cut ten cucumbers. Provence

roses blow against a wall. Dames violets very fine. Ten weeks stocks still in full beauty.' According to the 'chronicle of beer and wine', he tapped a barrel of his raisin wine the same day; its flavour, we learn, was 'very good'.

The *Naturalist's Journal* was compiled for his own use and satisfaction, and to be used by other naturalists, but was not written for publication. If only for this reason, even a complete 'year' is often by no means self-explanatory; records and comments made in the course of 1784 in many cases assume remarks made in earlier years, and in any year a knowledge of the topography and social structure of the village and parish is taken largely for granted. In this version of the 1784 *Journal* we have added not only pictures but a sub-text, therefore. At many points the *Journal*, though a distinct work from *Selborne*, throws light on the latter or else is amplified by it, and where appropriate references to *Selborne* have been included. ('TP' and 'DB' indicate, respectively, the letters to Thomas Pennant and those to Daines Barrington, published in *The Natural History of Selbourne*.) This is a slightly shortened version of the 1784 volume. Notably, the daily meteorological figures have been left out, though the comments accompanying these figures have in the main been assimilated to the dated entries.

White's spelling and punctuation have been left largely unchanged, but where he added something further to an entry at a later date (as with the extra note concerning Timothy the tortoise, May 28th), the addition is given in brackets. To touch on some details which may need clarifying for the present-day reader: White's temperatures are all in Fahrenheit, and '6 ae' means six pounds weight. (His '200 weight' would now be 'two cwt'.) The accident in which John Mulso was 'shot in the legs' (November 1st), cannot have been as bad as it sounds; Mulso was again staying with White for several days, some autumnal shooting was indulged in, and Mulso—inexpert in country matters—presumably received some stray pellets. The 'peace' White refers to on July 29th was that negotiated with France, among others, following upon the American War of Independence. His 'lights' were the glass-paned covers of his garden frames, although he can use the term also for the garden frames themselves; and the 'basons' he prepared were holes (basins) dug in various parts of the garden and filled with a mixture of loam and rotted dung, for plants which were unsuited to his own, predominantly chalky, soil. This still leaves many terms and usages for the reader to work out for himself. However, the place-names mentioned in the text—Gracious Street, Maiden Dance, the Short Lythe and so on—are all, I think, included in the map of eighteenth century Selborne.

The various private letters made use of in this introduction and in the sub-text are printed in either Rashleigh Holt-White's *The Life and Letters of Gilbert White* (1901) or Thomas Bell's edition of *The Natural History of Selborne* (1877). My thanks are due to the administrators of the British Library for allowing me access to the manuscript of the *Naturalist's Journal*; and I am grateful to the Selborne Society and the Ealing Central Library for permission to use books and papers from the Selborne Collection.

E.D.

A SELBORNE YEAR.
The 'Naturalist's Journal' for 1784.

JANUARY

Jan. 1.	(Selborne.) White fog. Snow in the night. Wagtails.
Jan. 2.	Rain. Swift thaw. Snow almost gone. The ground floated with water.
Jan. 3.	Vast storms of rain. Sun. Snow gone: flood at Gracious street.
Jan. 4.	Rain, rain. Wagtail.
Jan. 5.	Sun. Mild & pleasant.
Jan. 6.	Hard frost. Hoar frost lies all day.
Jan. 7.	Hard frost. Hoar frost lies all day, frost comes in a door. Dark & still.
Jan. 8.	Hard frost, small snow. Some wild-ducks up the stream near the village. Much wild fowl on the lakes in the forest.
Jan. 9.	Frosty. Dark & still. A grey crow shot near the village. This is only the third I ever saw in this parish. Some wild-geese near the village down the stream.

PIED WAGTAIL IN WINTER PLUMAGE.

Jan. 10.	Hard frost. Dark & still. Small snow on the ground. Mr Churton left us.
Jan. 14.	Showers, & strong gales.
Jan. 17.	Frost, sun. Snow-drops, & winter-aconites begin to blow.
Jan. 18.	Hard frost. Sun, sharp. Clouds put up their heads.

Jan. 19.	Severe frost. Sharp, driving snow.
Jan. 20.	Fierce frost. Drifted snow on the ground. Sun. Driving snow. Ice in chambers.
Jan. 21.	Fierce frost. Grey & sharp. Ice in chambers. Hares frequent the garden.
Jan. 22.	Hard frost. Snow. Snipes come up the stream.
Jan. 25.	Fierce frost. Bright & still. Much drifted snow still about. The turnips, that are not stacked, are all frozen & spoiled.
Jan. 26.	Fierce frost. Sun, grey. Made the *seedling-cucumber-bed* with two cart-loads of hot dung. Cut my last years hay-rick.
Jan. 27.	Considerable snow in the night. Grey & still. The hanger exhibits a very grotesque, & beautiful appearance.

CURLEW.

MAKING THE SEEDLING HOT-BED.
White was a specialist user of hot-beds and garden frames, particularly for cucumbers and melons: his cucumber seeds would be planted in a small 'nursery' bed during January, and the seedlings transplanted to a much larger 'fruiting' bed, made up with perhaps eight cartloads of dung, a month later. In 1784 he cut his first frame cucumber on May 5th. In earlier years he sometimes started the seeds at the beginning of January and cut the first cucumbers in mid-April—this quite without the aid of heated greenhouses.

Jan. 28.	Severe frost. Sun, sharp wind. Snow covers the ground, & hangs on all the trees, & shrubs.
Jan. 29.	Severe frost. Sun, & sharp wind. Frost within doors. The dung & litter freeze under the horses in the stable. The hares nibble off the buds on the espalier-pear-trees.
Jan. 30.	Severe frost. Sun. Grey & sharp. Ice in close chambers. A long-billed curlew has just been shot near the Priory. We see now & then one in very long frosts. Two, I understand, were seen.
Jan. 31.	Sharp frost. Sun. Snow melts on sunny roofs. Yellow wagtail on the Lythe. Much snow on the ground. Hares frequent my garden, & eat the stocks. Sowed some cucumber seeds.

Rain in Jan:—3 in: 18 h.

FEBRUARY

Feb. 1.	Severe frost. Cloudless, & sharp. Snow melts under hedges.
Feb. 3.	Fierce frost. Sun, & sharp wind. Much snow on the ground. Paths, & horse-tracks dusty. Cucumber seeds sprout. A near neighbour shot a brace of hares out of his window; & at the same discharge killed one, & wounded an other. So I hope our gardens will not be so much molested. Much mischief has been done by these animals.
Feb. 4.	Hard frost. Sun. Fleacy clouds, sky muddled. Paths thaw in the sun.
Feb. 5.	Rain. Swift thaw. Snow almost gone.
Feb. 6.	Hard frost. Sun & sharp air. Some snow remains. Sowed 48 bushels of peat-ashes on the great meadow, which covered more than half. 31 bush: were bought of my neighbours. Hail & sleet.
Feb. 7.	Hard frost. Sleet, & hail on the ground. Sun & clouds. Cutting wind. Snow.
Feb. 8.	Severe frost. Snow covers the ground. Sun, sharp wind.

SELBORNE, VIEW FROM ABOVE THE SHORT LYTHE.

The Short Lythe, now covered with mature beech trees, was a 'steep, rough pasture-field', as White knew it. From the flatter ground at the top of the bank, and facing south west, the visitor looked across Dorton and the Church Litten, where the Bourne and the Wellhead stream meet to become the Selborne stream, to the village and Selborne Down: Noar Hill lies to the east of Selborne Down, and the Selborne beech hanger covers the northern slope of the Down.

The 'yellow wagtails' White sometimes recorded in the parish in winter were without doubt grey wagtails in winter plumage. Confusing the two species—with no reliable recognition guides, and almost creating field ornithology as he went along—he could list the yellow, a summer visitor to this country, with his 'all the year round' birds, as he does in *Selborne*. (DB i)

Feb. 10.	Hard frost. No hares have frequented the garden since the man shot & killed one, & wounded an other. Snow.
Feb. 11.	Hard frost. Sun. Hare again in the garden.
Feb. 12.	Severe frost. Snow, wind. Deep snow.
Feb. 13.	Frost, snow, sun. Very deep snow much drifted. This evening the frost has lasted 28 days.
Feb. 14.	Sharp frost. Dark with haze. Sent Thomas as Pioneer to open the road to Faringdon: but there was little obstruction, except at the gate into Faringdon Hirn.
Feb. 15.	Fierce frost, snow. Snow deep, & drifted thro' the hedges in curious, & romantic shapes.
Feb. 16.	Hard frost. Grey. Snow deep. No hares frequent the garden.
Feb. 19.	Dark & still, grey, sun. Snow deep.
Feb. 20.	Dark & blowing. Snow. Much drifted snow.
Feb. 21.	White, warm fog. Small rain. Snow much wasted.
Feb. 22.	Deep fog. Rain. Snow melts, & the country is flooded. Flood at Gracious street.
Feb. 23.	Grey & mild. Sun, pleasant. The tops of the blades of wheat are scorched with frost. Crocus's swell for bloom. Snowdrops blow. Snow lies under hedges. Aurora borealis.

THOMAS HOAR AS PIONEER.
Conditions on the bridle-path to Faringdon were of
importance to White, because until October 1784 he was
still officiating curate at Faringdon, two miles to the south
west of Selborne. He would make the journey in almost
any weather, though during this winter he missed the
worst of the snow in his locality, being on a visit to his
brother Thomas at South Lambeth, during all of March.
Thomas Hoar was left in charge of the garden—and the
rain gauge.

Feb. 24.   (Alton.) Fog, wet, grey. The laurels, & laurustines are not injured by the severe weather. Snow scarce passable in Newton-lane!

Feb. 25.   (South Lambeth.) Wet, clouds, sun. Little snow on the road.

Feb. 27.   Clouds, strong gale. (Thomas Hoar kept an account of the rain at Selborne in my absence.) Filbert blows.

Feb. 28.   Dark, & harsh. Crocus's blow.

Feb. 29.   Dark, frost & ice.

Rain in February . . . 0 inc: 77 hund.

MARCH

Mar. 1.	Wh. frost, ice. Brother Tho: found a grass-hopper lark dead in his out-let. I was not aware that they were about in the winter.
Mar. 8.	Blustering, hail, showers.
Mar. 14.	Ice. Sun, & sharp wind.
Mar. 20.	Thick ice. Snow. Bright. Thermr: 29: at 9 in the morning.
Mar. 21.	Frost, ice. Deep snow at Selborne.
Mar. 22.	Frost, ice. Still. Roads very dusty.
Mar. 24.	Snow covers the ground. Snow gone.
Mar. 26.	Rain. Great snow at Selborne.
Mar. 28.	Frost, ice, blustering. Snow on hills & roofs.
Mar. 31.	Ice. Dark & harsh. Apricot begins to blow.
	Rain in March . . . 3 inch: 82 hund.

APRIL

Apr. 1.	Frost, ice. Sun, sharp.
Apr. 2.	(Selborne.) Dark & harsh. Thick ice on lakes & ponds. No snow 'till we came to Guild-down: deep snow on that ridge! Much snow at Selborne in the fields: the hill deep in snow! The country looks most dismally, like the dead of winter! A few days ago our lanes would scarce have been passable for a chaise.
Apr. 3.	Rain. The ever-green trees are not injured, as about London. The crocus's are full blown, & would make a fine show, if the sun would shine warm. (On this day a *nightingale* was heard at Bramshott!!)
Apr. 4.	Frost. Sun. Soft, & pleasant. The rooks at Faringdon have got young. Very little spring-corn sown yet. Wagtail. Snow as deep as the horses belly under the hedges in the North field. Snow melts.
Apr. 5.	Grey & mild. Small rain. My crocus's are in full bloom, & make a most gaudy show. Those eaten off by the hares last year were not injured. A brace more of hares frequenting my grounds were killed in my absence.

Apr. 6.	Rain. Snow. Apricots promise for a fine bloom. Persian Iris's blow. Dogs violets bud for bloom.

Apr. 7.	Dry & cold. Apricot begins to blow. Cucumber blows; female bloom without male. Snow melted. (A farmer told Mr Yaldon, that he saw *two swallows* on his way to Hawkley!!)

A very large fall of timber, of about 1000 trees, has been cut this spring in the *Holt-forest*; one fifth of which belongs to the Grantee Lord Stawel. He lays claim also to the lop & top: but the poor of the parishes of Binsted, & Frinsham, says it belongs to them; & have actually in a riotous manner taken it away. One man that keeps a team |

There was a rookery on the way to Faringdon church, at
'Farmer Pink's': April 4th was a Sunday.

has carryed home near forty stacks of wood. Forty nine of these people his Lordship has served with actions; & provided they do not make restitution, proposes to sue them. The timber, which is very fine, was winter-cut; viz: before barking time.

Apr. 8.	Grey. Sun. Men open the hills, & cut their hops. Red even.
Apr. 9.	Frost. Sun. *Swallow* seen near the forest. Many lettuces, both Coss, & Dutch, have stood-out the winter under the fruit-wall. They were covered with straw in the hard weather, for many weeks.
Apr. 11.	Wet & blowing. Ivy-berries are full-grown, & begin to turn black, & to ripen, notwithstanding the length of frost, & severity of the spring.
Apr. 12.	Snow: blowing, with hail-storms. Snow melted. Polyanths begin to blow. Violets blow.
Apr. 13.	Frost, ice, sun, hail storms. Mutton per pound 5d, veal 5d, lamb 6d, beef 4d, at Selborne.

THE 'LOP AND TOP RIOT'.

Traditional and manorial rights were still important in the Selborne parish and those surrounding it in White's time. Like Wolmer Forest, the Holt was a royal forest held by a grantee, but such estates too had been

'of considerable service to neighbourhoods that verge upon them, by furnishing them with peat and turf for their firing; with fuel for the burning their lime; and with ashes for their grasses; and by maintaining their geese and their stock of young cattle' (*Selborne*, TP vii)

At Selborne the villagers had fuel rights and the right to let their pigs into the woods for acorns and beech mast in the autumn. As a resident who had been born in the parish, White himself collected his fuel in October. Of the lop and top rioters, he writes later in the year that the writs have been served and that 'these folks, especially the females, are very abusive, and set my Lord at defiance'.

Apr. 14.	Rain, heavy snow! Much snow on the ground.

Apr. 15.	Fog. Sun. Dogs-toothed violets blow. Showers about. Snow gone. Crocus's make a splendid show. Bees gather much on the crocus's.

Dog's Tooth Violet, *Viola riviniana*.
The toothed stipules give the flower its local name.

Apr. 16.	White frost. Sun, showers. Crocus's begin to fall-off. Ring-dove builds in my fields. *Black-cap* sings. Nightingale heard in Maiden Dance. (Many swallows seen at Oak hanger-ponds; perhaps they were bank-martins.)

SUMMER MIGRANTS; SWALLOW, HOUSE MARTIN,
BLACKCAP, NIGHTINGALE, REDSTART.
In a letter to Molly, or Mary, White in mid-April, Gilbert asks, 'Pray how is it, Mrs Mary, that the present most *bitter* spring does not at all retard the coming of the summer birds?' That even the swallows and house martins were undeterred was of the greatest interest to him, as bearing on the argument over the migration-or-hibernation of the 'hirundine' species; where some other evidence seemed to favour the hibernation theory, 'first appearance' in cold weather, such as these of 1784, militated against it. Among the known hibernants watched carefully by White, the tortoise was slow to emerge this year; and as usual the bats appeared only when local temperatures reached 50°F.

Apr. 17.	Shower. Pleasant, & spring-like. The buds of the vines are not swelled yet at all. In fine springs they have shot by this time two or three Inches. Peaches, & Nectarines begin to blossom.
Apr. 18.	Sun, & clouds. Pleasant. Grass begins to grow a little on the grass-plots, & walks. Bank-martins at Bramshott.
Apr. 19.	Grey & mild. Timothy the tortoise begins to stir: he heaves up the mould that lies over his back. *Red-start* is heard at the verge of the highwood against the common.
Apr. 20.	Mild. Rain. No garden crops sowed yet with me; the ground is too wet. Artichokes seem to be almost killed.
Apr. 21.	Rain. Crocus's still make a figure. The wall-trees are coming into good bloom. Daffodils begin to blow. Two swallows about the street.
Apr. 22.	The spring backward to an unusual degree! Some swallows are come; but I see no insects except bees, & some phalaenae in the evenings. A *house-martin* at Newton-pond. Some black snails come out. Daiseys, & pile-worts blow.
Apr. 23.	Sun & clouds. Windy, shower. Swallows about. *Timothy* the tortoise comes forth from his winter-retreat.
Apr. 24.	Rain, hail, sun, & clouds. Strong gales all day. Planted ten rows of potatoes against the Wid: Dewye's garden. Planted one row in the best garden. John Carpenter buys now & then of Mr Plowlett of Rotherfield a chest-nut tree or two of the edible kind: they are large, & tall, & contain 60 or 70 feet of timber each. The wood & bark of these trees resemble that of oak, but the wood is softer & the grain more open. The use that the buyer turns them to is cooperage; because he says the wood is light for buckets, jets, &c: & will not shrink. The

grand objection to these trees is their disposition to be *shaky*; and what is much worse, *cup-shaky*: viz: the substance of these trees parts like the scales of an onion, & comes-out in round plugs from the heart. This, I know, was also the case with those fine chest-nut-trees that were lately cut at Bramshott-place against the Portsmouth-road. Now as the soil at Rotherfield is chalk, & at Bramshott, sand; it seems as if this disposition to be shaky was not owing to soil alone, but to the nature of that tree.

There are two groves of chestnuts in Rotherfield-park, which are tall, & old, & have rather over-stood their prime. J. Carpenter gives only 8d pr foot for this timber, on account of the defect above-mentioned.

Apr. 25.   Wh. frost. Sun & clouds, spring-like. Nightingale sings in my outlet. The *Cuckow* is heard in the hanger. Wheat grows & improves. Grass grows. No barley sown at Faringdon.

Apr. 26.   Dark & mild. Wet. Wagtail about. Sowed a crop of onions, & several sorts of cabbage: pronged the asparagus beds. Radishes grow. Crocus's out of bloom.

Apr. 27.   Dark & mild, rain. House-martin over my garden. One *Swift*.

Apr. 28.   Sun, clouds. Began mowing the grass-walks. Sowed a large crop of carrots in the great meadow. *Grass-hopper*-lark whispers. Many house-martins. One *swift*. Sweet even.

Apr. 29.   The hoar frost was so great, that Thomas could hardly mow. Sowed an other crop of carrots. One swift. Sweet after-noon. Bats out for the first time, I think, this spring; they hunt, & take the phalaenae along the sides of the hedges. There has been this spring a pretty good flight of wood-cocks about Liss. If we have any of those birds of late years, it has been in the spring, in their return from the west, I suppose, to the Eastern coast.

CHESTNUT TIMBER FOR JOHN CARPENTER.
Sequestered but relatively prosperous,

'The village of *Selborne*, and large hamlet of Oakhanger, with the single farms, and many scattered houses along the verge of the forest, contain upwards of six hundred and seventy inhabitants. We abound with poor; many of whom are sober and industrious, and live comfortably in good stone or brick cottages, which are glazed, and have chambers above stairs: mud buildings we have none.' (*Selborne*, TP v)

On the other side of the street from White's house stood the shops of John Carpenter the village carpenter, George Tanner the saddler and shoemaker, John Burbey the grocer and John Hale the butcher and slaughterman (in front of whose yard White planted the 'lime' trees). Beyond these was The Compasses—enlarged, it is now The Queen's Hotel—and beyond it, on the corner of Huckers Lane, was a blacksmith's forge. The village street could be described by White as a cart-way; it was difficult or impossible to bring a carriage into the village after prolonged rain, and in winter the narrow lanes of the parish were sometimes quite blocked with snow. The naturalist—who was not a carriage-owner—made his longer trips about the locality on a Galloway pony; he was a short, spare man, according to tradition.

Apr. 30.   Goose-berry bushes leaf: quicksets still naked. Pile-wort in full bloom. *Cucumbers* set, & swell. Polyanths begin to blow well. Tulips shoot, & are strong. Sowed a pint of scarlet kidney beans.

Rain in April . . . 3 inch. 92 hund.

LONG-EARED BAT.

MAY

May 1.	Sun, bright & cold, drying wind. Cucumbers set apace. Men pole hops; sow barley, & sow clover in wheat. Horse-chestnuts, & sycamores bud. Hyacinths blow. Made an annual hot-bed for four lights. Fine bloom on the wall-trees. Two swifts. Saw a cock *white-throat*.
May 2.	White frost, sun, & cold air. Flies come out. Several swifts: many house-martins.
May 3.	White frost. Mild. Roads dry very fast. The buds of hazels do but just open: so that the hedges are quite naked. Wall-cherries blow. Peaches, Nect. & Apricots finely blown. Earthed the annual beds. Set up a copper-vane (arrow) on the brew-house. No ring-ousels seen this spring: the severity of the season probably disconcerted their proceedings. Timothy the tortoise weighs 6 ae: 13 oun: he weighed at first coming out last year only 6 ae: $11\frac{1}{4}$ oun. He eat this morning the heart of a lettuce. Goody Hampton came to work in the garden for the summer.
May 4.	Fog, sun, summer weather. Ashes blow. Some beeches in the Short Lythe are bursting into leaf.

RING-OUZEL.
White had discovered—despite misinformation given him by Thomas
Pennant—that the ring-ouzel was a passage migrant in his region, going to
and from nesting sites in more northerly parts of Britain and perhaps in the
West Country. (His investigation of the species can be followed in *Selborne,*
TP xx, xxii, xxv, and DB vii.) Though in the cold spring of 1784 it was
notable by its absence, it usually appeared in the parish briefly in April and
then again at the beginning of October.

WEIGHING THE TORTOISE.

Timothy had been acquired by White in 1780, on the death of his aunt Rebecca, and was indulged (even by Thomas Hoar) but also studied. In a letter 'from the tortoise' to the young Hecky Mulso, he explains:

'you must know that my master is what they call a *naturalist*, and much visited by people of that turn, who often put on whimsical experiments, such as feeling my pulse, putting me in a tub of water to try if I can swim, etc.; and twice in the year I am carried to the grocer's to be weighed, that it may be seen how much I am wasted during the months of my abstinence, and how much I gain by feasting in the summer. Upon these occasions I am placed in the scale on my back, where I sprawl about to the great diversion of the shopkeeper's children.'

May 5.

Sun, sweet summer. Cut the first *cucumber*, a large one. The usual number of swifts do not yet appear. Apricots begin to set. Peaches, & nectarines blossom well. Sowed annuals in their frames. Red even.

May 6.

Vast dew, cloudless, summer. Sowed white cucumbers under an hand-glass. Sowed green cucumbers in the annual bed. Some beeches in the hanger begin to leaf. Pulled the first radishes. Crown-imperials, & fritillarias blown. The polyanths blow finely, especially the young seedlings from Bramshott-place, many of which will be curious. Shot three green-finches, which pull off the blossoms of the polyanths. Vine-buds swell. Pears promise much bloom. Apricots swell. There is a ring-dove's nest in the American Juniper in the shrubbery: but as that spot begins to be much frequented, the brood will scarcely come to good.

May 7.

Bright, summer, some flisky clouds. Beeches come out at a vast rate. Vines shoot. The early tulips blow. The number of swifts increased to 18, or 20. Owls have eggs.

May 8.

Windy. Dark & louring. Auricula's blow finely in the natural ground. Mountain-snow-drops in bloom. The hanger almost all green. Many trees in the Lythe in full leaf. Beeches on the common hardly budding.

May 9.

Brisk gale, sun hot. The hanger is very beautiful. Asparagus beds sprout. Curran-trees much blown; gooseberries moderately.

May 10.

Sun & clouds, hot, sprinkling. The wild cherry, vulg. called the *merris*, begins to blow. Plums blossom. Blackthorn begins to blossom. Fern-owl seen, but not heard. The black-birds, & thrushes are so reduced by the severe weather, that I have seen in my out-let only one of the former, & not one of the latter; not one missle-thrush. The ground is dry, & wants rain.

GREENFINCH AND POLYANTHUS.
The 'curious polyanths' were from Bramshott Place on the other side of Wolmer Forest, the home of the Mr Richardson who visited The Wakes in June, and whom White was to visit in September. He too was an enthusiastic gardener.

May 11.	Showers. Bright gleam. Cool. Sowed sweet alyssum in basons on the borders. Sowed dwarf kidney-beans, white: & one row of large white. Wheat improves very much: the women weed it.
May 12.	The hanger seems to be quite in leaf. Sowed an other row of large white kidney-beans. The leaves of some of the wall-trees begin to blotch already. Peaches & nectarines set. There seem to be two, if not three nightingales singing in my out-let. Small showers. Daffodils, crown-imperials, fritillarias fade.
May 13.	Hot sun. Cut the first bundle of asparagus. Wind cold on the down.
May 14.	Dark, rain. Sweet after-noon. Swallows build. They take up straws in their bills, & with them a mouthful of dirt. *Fern-owl* churs.
May 15.	Sun, summer. Cucumbers set apace: asparagus sprout. The bark of felled oaks runs remarkably well; so that the barkers earn great wages. The tortoise is very earnest for the leaves of poppies, which he hunts about after, & seems to prefer to any other green thing. Vines shoot, & show rudiments of bloom. Pears & cherries have much bloom. Such is the vicissitude of matters where weather is concerned; that the spring, which last month was unusually backward, is now forward. Spring-corn wants rain.

BEECHES: THE HANGER IN NEW LEAF.
White was a lover, and planter, of trees. He was particularly proud of a 'great spreading oak' which stood in front of his terrace, but he describes the beech as 'the most lovely of all forest trees, whether we consider it's smooth rind or bark, it's glossy foliage, or graceful pendulous boughs.' (*Selborne*, TP i) The windows of both his study and the parlour he added to the house looked out directly onto his garden and the Hanger.

SWALLOWS BUILDING.
White's papers on the swallow, house martin, sand martin
and swift—he assumed the four to be related, but had
reservations about including the swift—were read before
the Royal Society, and the hirundines, as he called them,
were among his bird favourites. The grace and diligence of
the swallow, in particular, intrigued him, and although he
accepted, or insisted on, 'migration in general', and made
perceptive suggestions as to its causes and function, and
while he set out the available evidence for and against
hibernation in some of the hirundine species fairly, the
notion that swallows and martins might 'slumber away'
the colder months was always somehow attractive to him.
(*Selborne*, DB ix, xxxvi)

May 16.	Great dew. Sun, sultry, summer. Apple-trees begin to blow. Scarlet kidney-beans are up. Tulips blow. So much sun hurries the flowers out of bloom! Left off fires in the parlor. Red even.
May 17.	Dew. Sun, cloudless. Flesh-flies begin to appear. Vast bloom of pears, & cherries! Cherries set. The spring-corn wants rain. Ground chops. Early tulips fade. The horses begin to lie out. Watered much.
May 18.	Cloudless. Hot, summer. Watered the fruit-trees, & crops. Sycamores blow, & smell of honey; & are much frequented by bees. Red even.
May 19.	Deep fog. Cloudless. *Fly-catcher* returns. This is the latest summer-bird, which never is seen 'till about the 20th of May. The Virginia creeper comes into leaf. Flowers fade, & go-off very fast thro' heat. There has been only one moderate shower all this month.
May 20.	Hot sun. Bats very busy at a quarter past three in the morning. Hops thrive; and have been tyed once to the poles. Bees thrive. Asparagus abound. Yellow even.
May 21.	Hot sun. Laurel & lilac blossom. Many apple-trees covered with bloom. Horse-chestnuts begin to blow. Apis longi-cornis appears over the grass-walks, in which it bores holes. Fern owl chatters.
May 22.	Cloudless, sun & gale. Columbines, & Monkshood blow. Lily of the valley blows. Began to tack the vine-shoots. Men bring up peat from the forest. Lapwings on the down.
May 23.	Sun, sultry. Field-crickets cry, & shrill in the short Lythe. Thunder-like clouds from S.W. to N.W.

May 24.   Gentle showers. Horse-chestnut finely blown. Apple-trees covered with bloom. A pair of swifts frequent the eaves of my stable. (These birds soon forsook the place, & did not build.)

SWIFTS.

May 25.   White dew. Sun, shower. Planted out the white cucumber plants under the hand-glasses. Planted some green cucumber plants in the frames among the bearing plants. Sowed some green cucumbers under the fruit-wall. Hawthorn, berberry, laburnum, mountain-ash, scorpionsena, guelder rose begin to blow. Honey-suckle against the wall begins to open. Lime-trees shew their bracteal leaves, & rudiments of fruit. Wall-nut trees shed their catkins, & shew rudiments of fruit. My great single oak shews many catkins. Distant thunder to the SE.

May 26.   Thunder in the night with heavy showers, & some hail. Grasshopper lark in my outlet.

COMPENSATION FOR THE LATE SPRING.
Flowers: Laburnum, Lilac, Guelder Rose, Lily of the Valley, Honeysuckle, Columbine, field bean, hawthorn, apple. Birds: lapwing, thrush, blackbird, grasshopper warbler, spotted flycatcher. Butterflies: brimstone, orange tip. The straying tortoise was at large for eight days, and was perhaps 'bent on amourous pursuits', White says.

[55]

May 27.	Sun & clouds. Brisk gale. Young red-breasts. St foin begins to blossom.
May 28.	Sun & clouds, showers about. Timothy the tortoise has been missing for more than a week. He got out of the garden at the wicket, we suppose; & may be in the fields among the grass. (Timothy found in the little bean-field short of the pound-field.) The nightingale, fern-owl, cuckow, & grass-hopper-lark may be heard at the same time on any evening in my outlet. Gryllo-talpa churs in moist meadows. Aphides appear on the shoots of the wall-cherries.
May 29.	No dew. Rain, sun. Flag-Iris, & Narcissus blow.
May 31.	Rain, dark. Cinnamon-rose blows.

Rain in May . . . 1 inch: 52 h.

JUNE

June 1.   Deep fog! Rain. Fraxinellas blow. The single white-thorn over the ash-house is one vast globe of blossoms down to the ground! Laburnums, berberries, &c: covered with bloom. Peonies in flower. Whitethorns covered with bloom every where.

June 2.   Sun & brisk gale. Flag-iris, & orange lily begin to blow. The forward wheat undulates before the wind.

June 3.   No dew. Dark with gale. Kidney-beans thrive, & are stuck. Corn looks finely. Turned the horses into Berriman's field. Pricked-out some good celeri-plants. Fiery-lily blows. Columbines make a fine show: this the third year of their blowing.

June 4.   Clouds & sun. Pricked-out annuals. A pair of fern-owls haunt round the zigzag. Sowed endive, first crop. Planted out annuals down the basons in the field.

June 5.   Blue mist. Sultry, vast drops. Distant thunder, vast hail!!! Much damage done to the corn, grass, & hops by the hail! Vast flood at Gracious street! vast flood at Kaker bridge! Hail near Norton two feet deep.
              Nipped-off all the rose-buds on the tree in the yard opposite the parlor window in order to make a bloom in the autumn. (No bloom succeeded.)

FIELD CRICKET.

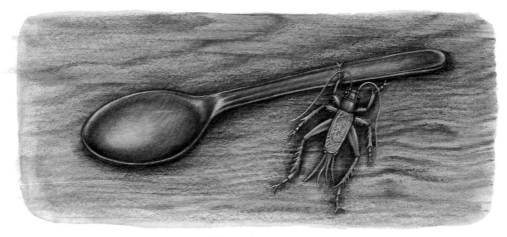

HOUSE CRICKET.

MOLE CRICKET.

The mole cricket, though now extremely rare, was common in the Selborne parish in the eighteenth century, on White's evidence. He made careful studies of field, mole and house crickets. They were good examples of 'congenerous creatures which live quite differently', a phenomenon he drew special attention to:

'While the *field-cricket* delights in sunny dry banks, and the *house-cricket* rejoices amidst the glowing heat of the kitchen hearth or oven, the *gryllus gryllo talpa* (the *mole-cricket*), haunts moist meadows, and frequents the sides of ponds and banks of streams, performing all it's functions in a swamp wet soil. With a pair of fore-feet, curiously adapted to the purpose, it burrows and works under ground like the mole, raising a ridge as it proceeds, but seldom throwing up hillocks.' (*Selborne*, DB xlviii)

'FERN-OWLS' OR NIGHTJARS OVER THE ZIGZAG.
White was preparing a paper on these 'curious, nocturnal, migratory birds' at the time of his death. He insisted that their churring note was produced only vocally; that the fern-own, churn-owl, eve-jar or puckeridge was not responsible for the disease in cattle also known as puckeridge (the true culprit was the warble fly); and that—despite another commonly held belief—the birds did not suck the teats of goats. The Zigzag, like the later 'bostal' path, had been constructed by White and his brothers.

June 6.	Rain. Sun, rain, thunder.

June 7.	The hail-storm which fell last Saturday was about a mile & a half broad, reaching from Wick Hill to the west end of the North Field. Had it been as extensive as it was violent, it would have ravaged all the neighbourhood. It seems to have originated in the parish of Harteley, & moved from N: to S. doing some considerable damage on Chilbury-farm. But the centre was over Norton Farm, where of course most harm was done. Grange farm which lies contiguous, to the S:, was much injured. Wick Hill farm on it's W: verge was pretty much cut. As the tempest advanced to the southward it soon spent itself: for the upper end of the village had scarce any hail at all; while the lower end, as far as the Plestor, sustained considerable loss from windows, & garden-frames. There fell at the same time prodigious torrents of rain on the farms above-mentioned, which occasion'd a flood as violent as it was sudden; doing great damage to the meadows, & fallows by deluging the one, & washing away the soil of the other. The hollow-lane by Norton was so torn & disordered as not to be passable 'till mended; rocks being removed that weighed 200 weight. The flood at Gracious street ran over the goose-hatch, & mounted above the fourth bar of Grange-yard gate. Those that saw the effect that the great hail had on ponds & pools say, that the dashing of the water made an extraordinary appearance, the froth & spray standing-up in the air three feet above the surface! The storm began with vast drops of rain, which were soon succeeded by round hail, & then by convex pieces of ice measuring 3 inches in girth. The rushing & roaring of the hail as it approached was truely tremendous. The thunder at the village was little & distant. (Tho' there was no storm that day at South Lambeth, yet was the air strongly electric, when the clouds were thin & light: for the bells of my Bro: Tho: White's electrical machine rung a great deal, & fierce sparks came from the machine.)

June 9.	Shower. Dark & louring. Continue to tack the vines. There is a show for much fruit.

The Hail-storm and Flood: the Barns at Grange Farm,
Seen from Gracious Street.

In the account of this violent storm given in *Selborne* (DB lxvi), White tells us that some of
his windows, and his garden frames, were smashed by the hail; early in 1785 he notes in
the *Journal*, 'Glazier's bill, £2-5-10 for garden-lights & hand-glasses.' (As we learn from
his account books, a working bricklayer, for example, might earn ten shillings a week.)
He followed the subsequent progress of the crops which had been lacerated by the hail
with close attention. A large part of the parish, and therefore some of the corn, hops and
peas, had been quite *un*affected by the storm. He could make useful comparisons here;
local events suggested many of his hypotheses and he was an investigating, as well as
observing, naturalist.

June 10.	Rain. Dark & blowing. Sold my St foin again to Timothy Turner; it looks well, & is in bloom. The 17th crop. The buyer is to cut it when he pleases.
June 11.	Rain in the night. Sun & clouds, blowing. The cherries against the walls begin to turn colour. The walks covered with leaves.
June 12.	Sun & clouds with strong gale. Men wash their sheep. Some wild straw-berries eatable. Finished tacking the vines. Hoed carrots, parsneps, &c. Received 5 gallons & a quart of French brandy from Mr Edmd: Woods.
June 13.	Sun & showers, with strong gales. Few hirundines appear; they are sitting on their eggs. Wheat comes into ear.

June 13.

On this day arrived here from India Mr Charles Etty. In his passage out, the ship he belonged to was burnt off the Island of Ceylon. He came back from Madras to the Cape of good hope in the Exeter man of war; & from thence worked his passage in the Content transport, which brought him to Spit-head. The Exeter was so crazy, & worn-out, that they broke her up, & burnt her at the Cape. Mr Ch: Etty brought home two species of Humming birds which he shot at the Cape of good hope; & two Ostriches eggs from the same place: two live tortoises from Madagascar: several fine shells from Joanna: & several turtle's eggs from the Isle of Ascension. Also the *Gnaphalium squarrosum*, a curious *Cudweed*, from a Dutch-mans garden at the Cape. Turtles-eggs are round, & white; a little variegated with fine streaks of red, & as large as the eggs of a kite; perhaps larger.

June 14.	Wet, fog on the hanger. The saint foin is in full bloom. Hoed & weeded the potatoes.
June 15.	Wet. Dark & still. Deep fog!! Cherries on the wall turn very fast. Apricots, peaches, & nect: swell. Continue to plant out annuals. Some swallows have young.

June 16.   Moist. Gale. Gleams of sun. Pears in abundance. *Phallus impudicus*, a stink-pot, comes up in Mr Burbey's asparagus-bed. Received an Hogsh: of port-wine, imported at Southampton. Thinned the crops of apricots, peaches, & nectarines, & pulled off many dozens.

STINK-POT FUNGUS, *Phallus impudicus.*
A surprise for John Burbey.

June 17.   Sun. Showers, blowing. Men sow turnips: a fine season. Elder-trees blow. Fine verdure on the down.

June 18.   Blowing, with small showers. Kidney-beans mount their sticks, & thrive. Roses blow.

June 19.   Showers. Men cut their St foin, & some clover.

June 20.   Cool, bright gleam. Narrow-leaved iris, corn flag, & purple martagons blow. Butter-fly orchis in the hanger.

June 21.   Dark & chilly. Rain. Standard honey-suckles in beautiful bloom. Cold & comfortless.

Some of White's Garden Flowers.
He mixed common and exotic varieties, and enjoyed bright colours; he dug 'basons' when he needed to quite replace his chalky soil. 1 Crown Imperial, *Fritillaria imperialis.* 2 Fritillary, *Fritillaria meleagris.* 3 Scorpion Senna (Crown Vetch), *Coronilla emerus.* 4 Guelder Rose (Viburnum), *Viburnum opulus.* 5 Fraxinella (Bastard Dittany), *Dictamnus fraxinella.* 6 Fiery Lily, *Lilium auratum.* 7 Columbine, *Aquilegia vulgaris.* 8 Flag Iris, *Iris pseudacorus.* 9 Purple Martagon (Turk's Cap Lily), *Lilium martagon.* 10 Standard Honeysuckle, *Lonicera xylosteum.* 11 Hemerocallis (Day Lily), *Hemerocallis viriola.* 12 Dame's Violet (Garden Rocket), *Hesperis matronalis.*

BUTTERFLY ORCHID, *Plantanthera chlorantha*.

June 22.	Heavy showers, strong gales. House-martins hatch.
June 23.	Blowing rain. St foin & clover lie in a bad state.
June 24.	Showers, dark & cold. Wheat in bloom. Bad weather for the blowing of wheat. Wheat looks poorly in the N: field. Continue to take up tulips, & to plant out annuals.
June 25.	Dark. Moist, & cold. Lighted a fire in the parlor. Planted out annuals. Turned-out the white cucumbers from under the hand-glasses.

HAND-GLASS OR GLASS CLOCHE.

June 26.	Dark & blowing, cold & wet. A brood of house-martins comes out. No swifts to be seen this cold blustering weather. Fire in the parlor.
June 28.	Grey, gleams. Showers about. *Vines* begin to blow. The ears of wheat are small. Wheat in bloom.

| *June* 29. | Dew, sun. Dark & soft. Cherries on the wall ripe & good. Mr & Mrs Richardson came. |
| *June* 30. | Grey. Sun. Showers about. |

The rain in June is—3 in: 65 h.

JULY

July 1.	Grey. Sun. Dark. Backward Orange-lilies, pinks, & cornflags, & backward honey-suckles begin to blow. Young *swallows* come out. Men house their clover.
July 2.	Dark & cold. Sun. Began to cut my meadow-grass: a good crop. Stopped down the vines which are in bloom. Mr & Mrs Richardson left us. Low creeping mists.
July 3.	Vast dew. Sun & clouds, warm. Continue to cut down the grass. Hay cut yesterday makes apace. Rye turns colour, & barley in ear round the forest. By the number of bank-martins round Oakhanger ponds, I should imagine that the first brood is out. Myriads of ephemerae near the ponds.
July 4.	Dew. Sun & clouds. Wheat in high bloom. Grass-hopper lark Whispers. Hemerocallis blows. On this day my Godson Littleton Etty discovered a young Cuckow in one of the yew hedges of the vicarage garden, sitting in a small nest that would scarce contain the bird, tho' not half grown. By watching in the morning we found that the owners of the nest were hedge-sparrows, who were much busied in feeding their great booby. The nest is in so secret a place that it is to be wondered how the parent Cuckow could discover it. Tho' the bird is very young, it is very fierce, gaping, & striking

HAYMAKING IN THE GREAT MEADOW.
White's garden and smallholding between them eventually covered the area now known as The Park. During the nineteenth century The Wakes, or Wakes as it was called originally, was greatly enlarged. But he himself added a one-storey 'great parlour' to the house (in 1777–78); before this he had levelled the terrace and built the ha-ha and fruit wall, and had added a shrubbery, an orchard and a large 'outer garden' to the garden as he inherited it. In this picture the great parlour is hidden by the oak-tree; the outer garden lay beyond the meadow and tall hedge, to our right.

at peoples fingers, & heaving up by way of menace, & striving to intimidate those that approach it. This is now only the fourth young cuckow that I have ever seen in a nest: three in those of h: sparrows, & one in that of a tit-lark.

As I rode up the N: field hill lane I saw young partridges, that were about two or three days old, skulking in the cart-ruts; while the dams ran hovering & crying up the horse-track, as if wounded, to draw off my attention.

July 5.

Vast dew. Clouds, sun. Scarlet kidney-beans blow. Hay makes finely. White cucumbers, under hand-glasses, begin to set. Timothy Turner cuts Bakers Hill, the crop of which he has bought. It is St foin run to seed, the 17th: crop. The garden looks gay with solstitial flowers.

SAINFOIN, *Onobrychis viciifolia.*
White grew this fodder crop anually from 1768 onwards; his sympathies were with 'enlightened' farming; but the 1784 crop was past its best by the time it was cut by Timothy Turner.

July 6.	Vast dew. Sun, cloudless. Cherries ripe, & finely flavoured. Ricked the hay of my great meadow in delicate order: six loads.
July 7.	Vast dew. Cloudless, very sultry. Finished my hay-rick in charming order: 1 load. By the manner of the swifts coursing round the church, it seems as if some of their young were out. Thunder & lightening, & much rain about.
July 8.	Dew. Hot. Much hay housed. Gloomy & heavy.
July 9.	Wet mist. Gleams. French marigolds begin to blow. Took away the cucumber-frames, & glasses. Beautiful yellow, & purple clouds in the N:W.
July 10.	Grey, & pleasant. Gale, sun. The hops damaged by the hail begin to fill their poles. Thatched my hay-rick. Cherries very fine. Grapes begin to set: vine leaves turn brown. The young cuckow gets fledge, & grows bigger than it's nest. It is very pugnacious. Cool.
July 11.	Sun & cool gale. Much hay about.
July 12.	Strong gale. Sun. White lilies blow. Hay makes finely. Lime-trees blossom. My horses, which lie at grass, have had no water now for about 8 weeks: nor do they seem to

YOUNG CUCKOO IN THE VICARAGE GARDEN.

White was born in the old vicarage, which stood on the site of the present vicarage next to the church, but never lived there in later life; he could not be vicar of Selborne, because he had gone to Oriel College, Oxford, and the Selborne living was administered by Magdalen College.

Recalling in *The Natural History of Selborne* the various bird species he has known to foster baby cuckoos, and naming the hedge-sparrow, meadow pipit ('tit-lark'), wagtail, whitethroat and robin, he suggests that the cuckoo chooses as birds on which to foist its eggs only species which will provide the young cuckoos with the appropriate insect food (*Selborne*, DB iv). In his day the idea was highly original.

desire any when they pass by a pond, or stream. This method of management is particularly good for aged horses, especially if their wind is at all thick. My horses look remarkably well.

July 13.

Great dew. Sun & gale. Finished ripping, furring, & tiling the back part of my house; a great jobb. Garden beans come in.

July 14.

Sun, dark, sun. Wheat turns colour. *Papilio Machaon* in Mrs Etty's garden. They are very rare in these parts.

July 15.

Cloudless. Golden weather. Tacked the wall trees. Trenched-out two rows of Celeri. Wood straw-berries, & cherries delicate!

July 16.

Bright. Dark & louring. Much wall fruit, many apples & pears. Made curran, & raspberry jam: the fruit is hardly ripe; but the small birds will steal it all away. Jasmine blows. White cucumbers swell.

July 17.

Sun. Gales & clouds. Scarlet kidney-beans show pods. Vines are out of bloom, & the grapes appear. Vine-leaves turn purple. Cut two white Cucumbers. Sowed a crop of white turnip-radishes. Mr Ch: Etty has taken the young Cuckow, & put it in a cage, where the hedge-sparrows feed it. No old Cuckow has been seen to come near it.

Mr Charles Etty brought down with him from London in the coach his two finely-chequered tortoises, natives of the island of Madagascar, which appear to be the *Testudo geometrica* Linn: & the *Testudo tessellata* Raii. One of these was small, & probably a male, weighing about five pounds: the other, which was undoubtedly a female, because it layed an egg the day after it's arrival, weighed ten pounds & a quarter. The egg was round, & white, & much resembling in size & shape the egg of an owl. The backs of these tortoises are uncommonly convex, & gibbous. Ray says of this species that the shell was 'Ellipticae seu ovatae figurae solidae plus quam dimidia

SWALLOWTAIL BUTTERFLY, *Papilio machaon*.
In August 1780 White recorded a swallowtail in his own
garden; it was the first he had seen in his district, he says,
but 'in Essex and Sussex they are more common'. The
(British) swallowtail can be found today only in restricted
parts of Norfolk.

CONVERSATION WITH CHARLES ETTY.

Charles Etty, a ship's officer and servant of the East India Company, was the son of the then vicar of Selborne and the father of Littleton Etty. White could listen at first-hand to the story of his recent adventures, and the young man brought down with him specimens calculated to please the naturalist-curate. (According to the quotation from John Ray, the shells of the Madagascar tortoises were 'in form like half an egg'.) White, if he thought of Selborne as in some respects a microcosm of the natural world, did not think that Selborne *was* the natural world. He corresponded with other naturalists, and through his brother John even exchanged information with Linnaeus. He enjoyed visits and journeys; he never left England—and did not reach the north of England—but as well as making his many local expeditions, he visited Oxford or London once or twice in the course of each year.

pars': Ray's quadrup: 260. The head, neck, & legs of these were yellow. These tortoises in the morning when put into the coach at Kensington were brisk, & well: but the small one dyed the first night that they came to Selborne; & the other, two nights after, having received, as it should seem, some Injury in their Journey. When the female was cleared of the contents of her body, a bunch of eggs of about 30 in number was found in her.

July 18.   Sun. Summer weather. Hops look remarkably well, & clear from vermin. The bar. has fallen for some days.

July 19.   Dark & blowing. Rain. The garden is finely watered.

July 20.   Showers. Strong gales all day. Saw an old swift feed it's young in the air: a circumstance which I could never discover before. Bro: Henry & his son Sam came.

July 21.   Dark. Rain. Cold & blowing. The cuckow in the cage dyed.

Gilbert White aligned himself with small and 'insignificant' creatures, and he describes their behaviour and relationships in precise detail. He seems to have felt quite confident on, and only on, his home ground, or within a parish which was itself a miniature world. But if he depended on 'Selbornian scenes', he thought of Selborne also as an outdoor laboratory; it was a microcosm, but one in which he could study species as well as particular plants and animals, and nature at large as well as his own Hampshire ecology.

July 22.	Cold & blowing. Showers. The wind broke off a great bough from Molly White's horse-chestnut tree.
July 24.	Sun. Dark & mild. Planted out some rows of polyanths from their seed-box. Planted out a bed of endive. Planted bore-cole, &c. Bro: Henry left us.
July 26.	Dark & still. Heavy rain. Bottled-out the hogshead of port-wine: my two thirds ran 16 dozen & four of my bottles, some of which are Bristol bottles, & therefore large. Many swifts about.

White also made his own beer and wine regularly. His strong beer, he remarks in a letter,

'is much admired by those that love pale beer, made with malt that is dryed with billet. My method is to make it very *strong*, and to hop very *moderately* at *first*; and then to put in it, at two or three times, half a pound at a time of *scalded* hops, before I tap it. This is the Wilts method, and makes the beer as fine as rock-water.'

A fortnight before he died—at seventy-three, an advanced age in the eighteenth century—he was at work in his garden.

July 27.	Rain in the night. Sun. Chilly. White cucumbers abound. Mr & Mrs Mulso, & Miss Mulso, & Miss Hecky Mulso came.

July 28.	Vast dew. Sun, clouds. First kidney-beans, scarlet. Artichokes.
July 29.	Heavy gales with rain. Trenched-out two rows of celeri. Drew-out from the port-wine hogsh:, for my share, eleven bottes more of wine: so that my proportion was 17 dozen, & three bottles. Thanks-giving for the peace.
July 30.	Showers in the night. Showers, gleams. Dark & chilly. Several swifts.
July 31.	Showers, sun. Several swifts. Potatoes come-in: they are very fine. Hops promise for a great crop: even those that were broken by the hail are much recovered, & may bear well.

Rain in July . . . 2:40.

AUGUST

Aug. 1.   Vast cold dew. Sun. Clouds. Pleasant afternoon.

Aug. 2.   Great dew, hot sun. Wheat-harvest begins. Several swifts. Wall-cherries, may dukes, lasted 'till this time: & were very fine. Sowed a crop of spinage, prickly-seeded, to stand the winter; & rolled the bed with a garden-roller. Sweet even.

Aug. 3.   Deep fog. Sun. Grey. Several swifts. Annuals now thrive: they never grew 'till lately. Vivid rain bow.

Aug. 4.   Dark & hot. Rain. Skimmed my two pasture fields. Young swallows, & martins congregate on the tower, & on dead trees. Some apricots begin to turn colour.

Aug. 5.   Sun. Soft air. Wet. Vast numbers of young martins, & swallows. Saw no swifts. Saw some nightingales in my outlet.

Aug. 6.   Dark, rain. There is fine aftergrass in my meadows. Blowing with heavy showers. Tremella abounds in the walks.

Aug. 7.   Sun & clouds. Shower. Many hop-poles are blown down. No swifts seen for some days. Cool, autumnal feel. Days much shortened.

Aug. 8.   Cold dew. Sun & clouds. Showers about. The wheat does not ripen: little of it cut: the reapers were stopped by the rain. Kidney-beans do not thrive, especially the white ones. Rain bows. No swifts.

SWALLOWS AND MARTINS OVER SELBORNE CHURCH.
Later in the year, in early and mid-October, hundreds of house martins in particular would gather on the church roof and tower, prior to their 'withdrawal'; and several pairs of swifts nested in the tower regularly. The swifts disappeared by mid-August—and White could have no doubt, therefore, that they were migrants. (Hibernation coincided with a 'defect of heat', he was sure.) But in August not only was the weather relatively warm; even in a 'bad' year, flying insects, the food of the hirundines, were still relatively plentiful. What, then, was the cause of the swift's departure? (*Selborne*, DB xxi, TP xxvi)

WHEAT HARVESTING: REAPING, BINDING, 'SHOCKING' AND CARRYING.

Farmers were largely at the mercy of the weather in the eighteenth century Selborne parish, and until the end of August 1784 the wheat harvest was repeatedly interrupted. White's journals show us too that agricultural crops and techniques were gradually changing in his region. He was largely responsible for a greatly increased growing of potatoes in the parish, and he refers to seed drilling (or sowing by machine) and the clamping (or stacking and covering) of turnips. 'Husbandry seems to be much improved at Selborne within these 20 years, & their crops of wheat are generally better', he suggests in 1781;

'not that they plough oftener, or perhaps manure more than they did formerly; but from the more frequent harrowings & draggings now in use, which pulverize our strong soil, & render it more fertile than any other expedient yet in practice.'

Again, in 1784 wheat ricks were appearing at Selborne; by 1790, according to White's records, the procedure—of stacking wheat after carrying and before threshing it, rather than 'housing' it in barns in the traditional but less efficient manner—was being widely adopted, at least by the larger farmers.

Aug. 10.	Rain. Showers, hot gleams. Harvest is interrupted by the wet. A pair of swifts. Mr: & Mrs Mulso, &c: left us.
Aug. 11.	Sun, clouds, sun. Wheat-harvest becomes general. The crop of spinage comes up finely. Turnip-radishes grow. Kidney-beans go off, & cucumbers do not thrive. They want heat. Pair of swifts.
Aug. 12.	Gleams. Moist, grey & hot. Wheat housing at Heards. Apricots begin to turn colour, & to look ruddy on the extremities of the trees. The wheat that was smitten by the hail does not come to maturity together: some ears are full ripe, & some quite green. Wheat within the verge of the hailstorm is much injured, & the pease are spoiled.
Aug. 14.	Grey. Sun, hot. Ants (flying) come from under the stairs, & fill the room, & windows. Much wheat housed this day. Plums show no tendency to ripeness. Scalded codlings come in. Annuals improve much. A puff-ball, lycoperdon bovista, was gathered in a meadow near Alton, which weighed 7 pounds, & an half, & measured in girth the longest way 3 feet two inches. There were more in the mead almost as bulky as this.
Aug. 15.	Vast dew! Cloudless. Sweet harvest weather. Some wheat-ricks made: & much wheat in shock. Some wheat not ripe. Women bring cran-berries, but they are not ripe. Ant-flies in my house very troublesome: they come from under the stairs. Thistle-down flies.
Aug. 16.	Brisk air. Hot sun. Pease are housed. Ripe apricots come in: very fine.
Aug. 17.	Dark & mild. Young swallows, & h: martins swarm, & cluster on trees, & houses. No swifts seen since the 11th. Much wheat this day housed. Pease are housed. Farmer Spencer, & farmer Knight are forced to stop their reapers, because their wheat ripens so unequally.

Aug. 18.

Dark & cold. Sharp wind. Fly-catchers abound. Wheat housed. The country is finely diversified by harvest-scenes. Spinage very thick on the ground. Men hoe turnips, stir their fallows, & cart chalk.

Aug. 19.

Strong gales in the night. Cold & winter-like. Wet. Sowed lettuces to stand the winter.

Aug. 20.

Rain, great rain all night. Lighted a fire in the parlor: the weather is very cold. (On this day my Niece Brown was delivered of her 4th child, a girl, which makes the 41st of my nephews & nieces now living.)

Aug. 21.

Showers, hail, thunder. The rain damages the apricots. Wheat lies in a sad, wet state: there is much abroad. Trenched celeri grows. Endives spread. Hops grow. Boiled up some apricots with sugar to preserve them.

Aug. 22.   Rain, dark & blowing. Men have not housed half their wheat. Apricots chop.

Aug. 23.   Sun & clouds. Strong gale. Preserved more apricots. Men turn their wheat in the grips. No wheat bound, or housed. Fly-catchers still. Low, white mist in the meadows. Vast dew.

Aug. 24.   Gleams. Dark & moist. The tops of beeches begin to be tinged. Much wheat bound. White turnip-radishes mild, & good, & large. Spinage bed thrives.

Aug. 25.   Shower. Dark & moist. Sad harvest weather. My great apricot tree appeared in the morning to have been robbed of some of it's ripe fruit by a dog that had stood on his hind legs, & eaten-off some of the lower apricots, several of

STEALING THE APRICOTS.
White was to pick apricots steadily until the first week in
September, the 'late bad season' notwithstanding and
although they began to 'chop' (or crack). Preserving and
jam-making were to be taken seriously, as was the birth of a
new nephew or niece.

which were gnawn, & left on the ground, with some shoots of the tree. On the border were many fresh prints of a dogs feet. I have known a dog eat ripe goose-berries, as they hang on the trees.

Aug. 26.   Dark & cold. Gale. This proves a very expensive, & troublesome harvest to the farmers. Wheat begins to grow as it lies. Pease suffer much, & will be lost out of the pod. Tyed-up some endives, & planted-out some. Wheat turned, but none bound. Milder.

Aug. 27.   Sun & clouds. Louring. Field-turnips grow. Celeri grows. Wheat bound, & some housed.

Aug. 28.   Rain. Grey with gale. Autumnal crocus, colchicum, blows. Men house wheat. Some thunder. Preserved more apricots. Young martins in a nest under the eaves of my stable. Many wallnuts on the tree over the stable: the sort is good but the tree seldom bears.

Aug. 29.   Sun & clouds. Pleasant, sprinkling. Much wheat abroad. Much tremella on the ground. A Faringdon man shot a young fern-owl in his orchard.

Aug. 30.   Vast dew. Sun & Clouds. Dark. Peaches & nectarines swell & grow, but want warm, dry weather to ripen them, & give them flavour. Grapes are very backward. Wheat carted all day. Swallows gather on the tower.

Aug. 31.   Rain, sun and clouds. Fine afternoon. Fly-catchers still. No wheat housed. Many pease abroad, that have lain for weeks. Heavy clouds on the horizon.

The rain in August was . . . 3 inch: 88 h.

SEPTEMBER

Sept. 1.   Deep fog. Gleams of sun. Swallows gather on the tower. Wheat housed. Farmer Town began to pick his hops: the hops are many, but small. They were not smitten by the hail, because they grew at the S.E. end of the village. Hopping begins at Hartley.

The two hop-gardens, belonging to Farmer Spencer & John Hale, that were so much injured, as it was supposed, by the hail-storm on June 5th shew now a prodigious crop, & larger & fairer hops than any in the

HOP GARDEN AND HOP-PICKING.

In a good hop harvest 'a woman and her girl' could pick twenty or more bushels in a day, at a penny ha'penny a bushel; but hops were a notoriously variable crop, and frequently failed altogether. The hop is dioecious, and White advised leaving male as well as female plants in the hop fields. In September 1784 he was more interested in uneven growth due to another cause: the pruning effect, as it might be termed, of the freak hail-storm. To the surprise of the growers, and while the corn which had been damaged in June was never to recover fully, the slashing off of their uppermost shoots had the opposite effect on the hop plants. Writing to Molly at the end of August, he says, 'Please to send me a good large ham. Neighbour Hale and I have been both walking in his hop-garden, and in the contiguous one of Spencer, both of which were smitten by the hail: and we both agree that the seeming calamity of the hailstorm has proved a great advantage to each owner.' At this time the use of wires and strings in hop cultivation had yet to be introduced in this country—and hop poles might be blown down.

parish. The owners seem now to be convinced that the hail, by beating off the tops of the binds, has encreased the side-shoots, & improved the crop. Que: therefore, should not the tops of hops be pinched-off when the binds are very gross, & strong? We find this practice to be of great service with melons, & cucumbers.

The scars, & wounds on the binds, made by the great hailstones, are still very visible.

Sept. 2.

Grey, mild. Sun & clouds. Fine harvest weather. Timothy comes forth into the walks. The weather has been so cold that he has not been out for some time. Much wheat housed. Harvest moon.

Sept. 3.

Grey, mild. Hot sun. China-asters begin to blow. Saw a *white-throat* in the garden. Sweet harvest weather. Wheat ricked, & housed. Mich: daisies begin to open. Many *uncrested wrens* still appear.

My Nep: Edmd: White & Mr Clement launched a balloon on our down, made of soft, thin paper; & measuring about two feet & an half in length, & 20 inches in diameter. The buoyant air was supplyed at bottom by a plug of wooll wetted with spirits of wine, & set on fire by a candle. The air being cold & moist this machine did not succeed well abroad: but in Mr Yalden's stair-case it rose to the ceiling, & remained suspended as long as the spirits continued to flame, & then sunk gradually. These Gent. made the balloon themselves. This small exhibition explained the whole balloon affair very well: but the position of the flame wanted better regulation; because the least vacillation set the paper on fire.

Sept. 4.

Vast dew. Cloudless, golden weather. Wheat will be finished off to day pretty well. Fly-catchers seem to be withdrawn. Swallows cluster on the cherry-trees at the parsonage. Tyed-up more endive: endive very large. Antflies swarm.

Sept. 5.

Vast dew. Sun, sultry. No wasps yet: no mushrooms appear. One *fly-catcher* at Faringdon. Annuals begin to make a great show. Heavy clouds about.

TIMOTHY IN THE GARDEN.

The tortoise was a true weather gauge throughout the year; he—though it seems now, from the carapace still preserved in the Natural History Museum, that Timothy was female—disliked both cold and rain. The visit to Selborne of White's friend John Mulso and his daughters in late July resulted in a letter in verse from Hecky Mulso to Timothy; and in reply White wrote the *Letter from Timothy the Tortoise to Miss Hecky Mulso*. It gives a fictitious early history of the 'sagacious reptile': 'in my present situation', the tortoise goes on, 'I enjoy the range of an extensive garden, abounding in lettuces, poppies, kidney beans, and many other salubrious and delectable herbs and plants, and especially with a great choice of delicate gooseberries.' He, or she, is now identified as a *Testudo graeca*.

SWALLOWS IN THE CHERRY TREE.
While the martins often congregated on rooftops, 'the swallows seem to delight more in holding their assemblies on trees'.

Sept. 6.   Great dew. Hot, cloudless. Grapes begin to turn; but the bunches are small & mean. Peaches & nectarines swell, & redden, & advance towards ripeness. Hopping becomes general.

Sept. 7.   Deep fog. Golden weather. The crop of apricots, which was very great, is over. Ant-flies swarm from under the stairs. I saw lately a small Ichneumon-fly attack a spider much larger than itself on a grass-walk. When the spider made any resistance the Ichneumon apply'd her tail to him, & stung him with great vehemence so that he soon became dead, & motionless. The Ich: then running backward drew her prey very nimbly over the walk into the standing grass. This spider would be deposited in some hole where the Ich: would lay some eggs: & as soon

ICHNEUMON AND GARDEN SPIDER.
White was not an insect specialist, but the precise detail of the insect world delighted this 'prince of personal observers'; like Jean Henri Fabre, he thought 'a close and loving study of insect life' much more important than 'arranging pretty beetles in a cork box'. As a gardener and smallholder, he believed also in the control of 'noxious' insects, but even this, he insisted, should be based on a careful examination of the 'life and conversation' of the creatures in question; the true naturalist familiarized himself with his subjects' 'manners'—or habits.

as the eggs were hatch'd, the carcase would afford ready food for the maggots. Perhaps some eggs might be injected into the body of the spider in the act of stinging. Some Ich: deposit their eggs in the aureliae of butterflies, & moths.

Sept. 8.　Vast white dew. Hot sun. Sultry, golden weather. H: martins congregate in vast flocks. Fine hopping: the poor earn good wages. Men house barley in fine order. No wasps are seen.

Sept. 9.　Fog. Sun, sultry, cloudless. Blanched endive comes-in. Some peaches: but not fine. *Fern-owl.*

Sept. 10.　(Bramshott place.) Dark & sultry. *Uncrested wrens* seem to be withdrawn. Mr Richardson's wallfruit at Bramshott-place is not good-flavoured, nor well-ripened: & his vines are so injured by the cold, black summer, as not to be able to produce any fruit, or good wood for next year. Mr Dennis's vines at Bramshott also are in a poor state.

Sept. 11.　(Selborne.) Great dew. Sun, sultry. Mr Randolph the Rector of Faringdon, came.

Sept. 12.　Dew. Heat, cloudless. Peaches, & nectarines advance towards ripeness. Several hornets, but no wasps. Ground dry, & heated.

Sept. 13.　Vast dew. Cloudless, sultry. Some few wasps. Young martins in a nest under the eaves of my stable. Peaches, & nectarines come in. Turned the horses in the little meadow for the first time since it was mowed. There is good after-grass.

Sept. 14.　Sun. Fog. The heats are so great, & the nights so sultry, that we spoil joints of meat, in spite of all the care that can be taken. My grapes turn very fast.

Sept. 15.   Grey. Hot sun. Air. Peaches & nectarines not delicate. Mr Randolph left us. Grass-walks burn. The autumn-sown spinage turns out a fine crop: but is much too thick. We draw it for use.

WALL FRUIT: NECTARINES AND PEACHES.

Almost all White's fruit eventually cropped heavily in 1784; the grapes which seemed at first to be 'not delicate' were well flavoured later in October. For once, moreover, his fruit was altogether superior to that of the much grander Bramshott Place, the home of his friend Richardson. On a sandy loam and lying in a river valley, the Bramshott garden usually produced 'an abundance of everything'. His own soil dried hard in summer and was stiff and heavy in winter unless it was regularly treated and 'ameliorated': as he notes ruefully after a visit to Bramshott, 'sandy soil much better for garden-crops than chalky'.

Sept. 16.	Cold dew. Hot sun. Martins cling, & cluster in a very particular manner against the wall of my stable & brew-house: also on the top of the may-pole. This clinging, at this time of year only, always seems to me to carry somewhat significant with it. Grapes come in. Grapes well-flavoured, the late bad season considered. Necta-rines good. Endives run to seed.
Sept. 17.	Vast dew. Clouds, hot sun. Nep. Ben White left me: he stayed a few days. Tyed-up more endive. Ivy begins to blow. Sweet autumnal weather.
Sept. 18.	Deep fog. Sun, broken clouds. Nectarines very good. Bees begin to devour the nectarines. Endives very fine. Sweet even.
Sept. 19.	Great dew. Sun, sultry. Cloudless. The wind turns up the leaves of the trees. Dark weather to the S:W.
Sept. 20.	Heavy showers, grey. Uncrested wren still appears. Hopping in general is finished, except in some few gardens.
Sept. 21.	Dew. Sun, clouds, shower. Harvest mostly finished. Gathered-in the early pippins, called *white apples*: a great crop. Showers about. Peaches, & nectarines are good.
Sept. 22.	Rain, gleams, hot, rain. Wall-fruit falls off. We keep drawing the spinage, which is grown very large, & much too thick. Endives very large, & fine. Many hirundines.
Sept. 23.	Rain. Hot sun. Showers about. Hirundines, some.

APPLE-PICKING AT SELBORNE.
Apples were sold for only eight pence a bushel, where a bushel of apples would weigh perhaps forty pounds. In the midst of this fruit picking White notes briefly that on September 29th he became permanent curate at Selborne: the Rev. Andrew Etty had died, and Mr Taylor, the new vicar, did not intend to be resident.

Sept. 25.	Sun. Vast showers. Swallows. Thunder. Sister Henry White, & her daughter Lucy came. Peaches & Nect: rot very fast.
Sept. 26.	Heavy showers. Corn out at Faringdon & Chawton. Mr Taylor took possession of Selborne vicarage.
Sept. 27.	Sun & clouds. Showers. Hirundines.
Sept. 28.	Small shower. Sun, clouds. Grapes good. Hirundines. Peaches & nect: watery & rotten.
Sept. 29.	Vast dew. Sun. Bright & pleasant. Took possession of Selborne curacy. Oats & barley much grown. Hirundines.
Sept. 30.	White frost. Sun, pleasant. Hirundines, a few. Some wasps. Men house oats. Fire in the parlor.

Rain in September . . . 2 inch: 51 h.

OCTOBER

Oct. 1.	White frost. Sun, pleasant. Gathered-in the Swan's egg, autumn-burgamot, Cresan-burgamot, Chaumontelle, & Virgoleuse pears; a great crop. The Swan-eggs are a vast crop. Some swallows. A wood-cock was killed in Blackmoor Woods: an other was seen the same evening near Hartley-wood.
Oct. 2.	White frost. Grey & mild. Men house beans, & oats. Many house-swallows.
Oct. 3.	Grey, still & cool. Some h: swallows. Two young men killed a large *male otter*, weighing 21 pounds, on the bank of our rivulet, below Priory long mead, on the Hartley-wood side, where the two parishes are divided by the stream. This is the first of the kind ever remembered to have been found in this parish.

Overleaf:
DORTON AND THE LONG AND SHORT LYTHES, FROM THE END OF HUCKERS LANE.
This was one of White's favourite Selborne 'prospects'. He would go to the Short Lythe on warm summer afternoons to study the field crickets, and it was here that Farmer Spencer's cow rolled from the top of the hill to the bottom without coming to any harm. Selborne stream passes in front of Dorton cottage, and one of his regular walks was along the valley of the stream. A path ran from Dorton cottage to Priory Farm and Oakhanger; though from Huckers Lane the more direct way was along the ancient *via Canonorum*, through Dorton woods and under Sparrow's Hanger, a small property owned by White and containing some fine beech trees.

Oct. 5.   Grey. Sun. Soft & still. Swallows. Gathered in the knobbed russets, & the Cadilliac pears.

Oct. 6.   Fog. Sun, pleasant. The ground is very dry. A vast flock of ravens over the hanger: more than sixty!

Oct. 7.   Dew. Sun, sharp wind. Some swallows. Pronged-up potatoes, & carrots, a fine crop. Mrs Harry White, & Lucy left us.

It has been the received opinion that trees grow in height only by their annual upper shoot. But my neighbour over the way, Tanner, whose occupation confines him to one spot, assures me that trees are expanded & raised in the lower parts also. The reason that he gives is this; the point of one of my Firs in Baker's Hill began for the first time to peep over an opposite roof at the beginning of summer; but before the growing season was over, the whole shoot of the year, & three or four joints of the body beside became visible to him as he sits on his form in his shop. This circumstance will be worthy of attention an other year. According to this supposition a tree may advance in height considerably, tho' the summer-shoot should be destroyed every year.

Oct. 8.	Dew. Sun, pleasant. Sharp wind. Some few swallows. Dug-up the carrots, & potatoes. Mr Richardson came.
Oct. 9.	Cold dew. Sun, sharp wind. Some few swallows. Mr R: left us. A person took a trout in the stream at Dorton, weighing 2 pounds, & an half; a size to which they seldom arrive with us, because our brook is so perpetually harassed by poachers.
Oct. 10.	Dark. Heavy & still. Began to turn my horses into the great mead, for the first time since it was mowed. The head of grass is great.
Oct. 11.	Cold dew. Sun. Gale, sweet afternoon. Men draw, & stack turnips. Ravens, many.
Oct. 12.	Fog. Sun. Dark & still. Grapes are very fine. My well is very low in water.
Oct. 13.	Dark, sprinklings. Two or three swallows. Gathered the dearling-apples in the meadow; a great crop.
Oct. 14.	Grey & cold. Sun, sharp wind. Finished gathering in the apples. Apples are in such plenty, that they are sold for 8d per bushel. Planted coss-lettuce, & Dutch, in rows under the fruit-wall, to stand the winter.
Oct. 15.	White frost. Sun & sharp air. Leaves fall. The foliage of trees is much tinged. Potatoes, & carrots abound. Timothy retreats under the laurel hedge.
Oct. 16.	Fog. Sun, but some haze. Wall-nuts on the best tree not good. Mr Blanchard passed by us in full sight at about a quarter before three P:M: in an air balloon!!! He mounted at Chelsea about noon; but came down at Sunbury to permit Mr Sheldon to get out; his weight over-loading the machine. At a little before four P:M: Mr Bl: landed at the town of Romsey in the county of Hants.

BLANCHARD'S BALLOON.

Somewhat longer versions of the letter White sent to a newspaper—the newspaper cutting is pasted into the manuscript *Journal*—were posted to Anne, his sister, and, of course, Molly at South Lambeth. He believed that science could be humane and constructive, and welcomed much of the technical change he met with; but at the end of his letter to Molly the importance of Blanchard's balloon is overtaken by another concern. He was expecting a visit from his niece. She and her father, Thomas White, had been delayed earlier in the year, and Gilbert tells her, 'We most earnestly hope to see you soon, and shall rejoice more at the sight of your post chaise, than if the balloon had settled on our sheep-down.'

Extract of a Letter from a Gentleman in a village fifty miles S.W. of London, dated Oct. 21.

'From the fineness of the weather and the steadiness of the wind to the N.E. I began to be possessed with a notion last Friday, that we should see Mr. Blanchard the day following, and therefore I called upon many of my neighbours in the street, and told them my suspicions. The next day proving also bright and the wind continuing as before, I became more sanguine than ever; and issuing forth, exhorted all those who had any curiosity to look sharp from about one to three o'clock, as they would stand a good chance of being entertained with a very extraordinary sight. That day I was not content to call at the houses, but I went out to the plow-men and labourers in the fields, and advised them to keep an eye at times to the N. and N.E. But about one o'clock there came up such a haze that I could not see the hill; however, not long after the mist cleared away in some degree, and people began to mount the hill. I was busy in and out till a quarter after two, and in taking my last walk observed a long cloud of *London smoke* hanging to the N. and N.N.E. This appearance encreased my expectation. At twenty minutes before three there was a cry that the balloon was come. We ran into the orchard, where we found twenty or thirty neighbours assembled, and from the green bank at the end of my house, saw a dark blue speck at a most prodigeous height dropping as it were out of the sky, and hanging amidst the regions of the air between the weather-cock of the Tower and the Maypole: at first it did not seem to make any way, but we soon discovered that its velocity was very considerable, for in a few minutes it was over the Maypole, and then over my chimney, and in ten minutes more behind the wallnut-tree. The machine looked mostly of a dark blue colour, but sometimes reflected the rays of the sun. With a telescope I could discern the boat and the ropes that supported it. To my eye the balloon appeared no bigger than a large tea-urn. When we saw it first it was north of Farnham over Farnham Heath; and never came on this (east) side the Farnham road; but continued to pass on the N.W. side of Bentley, Froil, Alton, &c. and so for Medstead, Lord Northington's at the Grange, and to the

right of Alresford and Winchester. I was wonderfully struck with the phaenomenon, and, like Milton's "Belated Peasant", felt my heart rebound with joy and fear at the same time. After a time I surveyed the machine with more composure, without that concern for two of my fellow creatures; for two we then supposed there were embarked in that aerial voyage. At last seeing how securely they moved, I considered them as a group of cranes or storks intent on the business of emigration, who had

> Set forth
> Their airy caravan, high over seas
> Flying, and over lands, with mutual wing
> Easing their flight.'

Oct. 17.	Great dew. Sun. Still. Fine mackerel sky.
Oct. 18.	Great dew. Fog. Sun. This day the dry weather has lasted three weeks.
Oct. 19.	Sun & clouds. Sweet afternoon. Many spider's webs.
Oct. 20.	White frost. Dark & heavy. Wall-nuts innumerable, but few good. Foliage of trees fades very fast, & becomes much tinged, & dusky.
Oct. 21.	Frost, ice. Sun, pleasant. This day at 4 o'clock P:M: Edmd: White launched an air-balloon from Selborne Down, measuring about 8 feet & $\frac{1}{2}$ in length, & 16 feet in circumference. It went off in a steady & grand manner to the E. & settled in about 15 minutes near Todmoor on the verge of the forest.
Oct. 22.	Clouds, some drops. Sun, mild. Ash-trees are stripped of their leaves. My hedges beautifully coloured.
Oct. 23.	Shower. Sun & clouds. Celeri comes in. *Red-wings* on our common. Leaves fall very fast. Rooks carry-off the wall-

THE SECOND SELBORNE EXPERIMENT.

Edmund was the son of Gilbert's brother Benjamin, and at this time was curate at Newton Valence; the Whites were scientifically minded as a family—though all except Gilbert were amateurs. This second and much larger Selborne balloon was launched from the top of the Down, above the Zigzag.

nuts. I have seen no ants for some time, except the Jet-ants, which frequent gate-posts. These continue still to run forwards, & backwards on the rails of gates, & up the posts, without seeming to have any thing to do. Nor do they appear all the summer to carry any sticks or insects to their nests like other ants.

Oct. 24.   White frost. Sun, cold wind, shower. Leaves fall much. Grapes very fine. Timothy retires under the laurel hedge, but does not bury himself.

Oct. 25.   Hard frost. Thick ice. Snow! In my way to Newton I was covered with snow! Snow covers the ground, & trees!!

Oct. 26.   Grey. Sun, sharp wind, shower. Horses begin to lie within. Compleated three rows of lettuces the whole length of the fruit-wall, to stand the winter.

Oct. 27.   Hard frost. Sun, shower. Dunged, trenched, & earthed the asparagus-beds, & filled the trenches with leaves, flower-stalks, &c. Timothy retires under the laurel hedge, & begins to bury himself.

Oct. 28.   White frost. Moist, sharp wind. Rooks carry off wall-nuts. Mr John Mulso came.

Oct. 29.   Sun. Grey & mild. Grapes very fine. Foliage turns very dusky: the colour of the woods & hangers appears very strange, & what men, not acquainted with the country, would call very unnatural.

Oct. 30.   Soft rain. Grey & mild. Bat comes out.

Oct. 31.   Grey, still & soft. Many people are tyed-up about the head on account of tooth-aches, & face-aches.

Rain in October . . . 0 inc: 39 hund.

NOVEMBER

Nov. 1.	Rain. Grey & mild. Mr John Mulso was shot in the legs.
Nov. 2.	Rain, mild. Leaves fall very fast. Grapes delicate. Bats are out early in the evening, hunting for gnats, before moths begin to flie.
Nov. 4.	Grey & mild. Sun, pleasant. Timothy out. Great meteor.
Nov. 5.	Grey. Mild & still. Wet. The deep, golden colour of the larches amidst the dark evergreens makes a lovely contrast!
Nov. 7.	Sun & clouds, cold shower. Timothy out. Jet-ants still appear.
Nov. 8.	Hard frost. Sun, pleasant. The hanger almost naked: some parts of my tall hedges still finely variegated: the fading foliage of the elm is beautifully contrasted to the beeches!
Nov. 9.	Frost, rain. Leaves fall very fast.
Nov. 10.	Sun. Warm haze. Mr John Mulso left us.

Nov. 11.	Blowing all night. Rain. Picked-up the beech mast which fell from the trees of my planting, & sowed it in the thin parts of the hedges of Baker's Hill. Trees & hedges are naked. Jet-ants out still.
Nov. 12.	Much rain in the night. Rain, sun. Many grapes left: grapes delicate, but the vines have lost all their leaves.
Nov. 13.	Grey. Sun, pleasant. Gathered-in the remaining grapes: a large crop. Timothy comes out.
Nov. 14.	Dark & mild. Wet. No acorns, & very few beech-mast. No beech-mast last year, but acorns innumerable.

During the previous October White had remarked in the
Journal,

'If a masterly lands-cape Painter was to take our
hanging woods in their natural colours, persons . . .
would object to the strength & deepness of the tints, &
would pronounce, at an exhibition, that they were
heightened & shaded beyond nature.'

Nov. 15.	Stormy in the night. Rain.
Nov. 17.	Vast showers with hail. Bright & chill.
Nov. 18.	Dark & mild. Rain. Timothy out. (In the evening he retired into the laurel hedge, & has not been seen since.) Very wet, & blowing.
Nov. 20.	Hard frost. Sun. Large fieldfares appear.
Nov. 22.	Hard frost. Swift thaw, rain. Finished sweeping up the leaves in the walks.
Nov. 23.	Frost. Deep fog. Sun. Brother Thomas, & his daughter, & two sons came. The chaise that brought some of them passed along the king's high road into the village by Newton lane, and down the N: field hill; both of which have had much labour bestowed on them, & are now very safe. This is the first carriage that ever came this way. Planted tulips against the borders; & the small off-sets in a nursery-bed.
Nov. 25.	Rain & wind. Sun, pleasant. The dew on the out-side of windows.
Nov. 26.	Grey. Still & mild. Haws in such quantities that they weigh down the white-thorns.
Nov. 27.	Grey & mild. Flesh-flies come forth. Beetles flie.

MOLLY ARRIVES AT LAST.
Like his father and grandfather before him, White encouraged attempts to improve the parish roads, or lanes; he himself had a pavement laid in the village street. At this time there was no direct road from Alton to Selborne, and he had sent Molly and her father detailed instructions on how to find this 'new road', the improved North Field lane, into the village.

Nov. 29.	Cold & wet. Wood-pigeons in small flocks.
Nov. 30.	Fog. Sun, pleasant.

Rain in November . . . 4 inch: 70 huns.

HAWS ON WHITETHORN OR HAWTHORN.

DECEMBER

Dec. 1.	Rain in the night. Frost, sun, cold air.
Dec. 2.	Hard frost. Sun, pleasant. Timothy is buried we know not where in the laurel-hedge.
Dec. 5.	Dark, rain.
Dec. 6.	Rain, & hail. Dismally dark: no wind with this very sinking glass.
Dec. 7.	Snow, snow, snow.
Dec. 8.	Fierce driving snow all day. Much snow drifted. Siberian weather.
Dec. 9.	Vast snow in the night. Frost, bright sun. Snow 16 inches deep on my grass-plot: about 12 inches at an average. Farmer Hoar had 41 sheep buried in snow. No such snow since Jan: 1776. In some places much drifted.
Dec. 10.	Extreme frost!!! yet still bright sun. Thomas Hoar shook the snow carefully off the evergreens. The snow fell for 24 hours, without ceasing. The ice in one night in Gracious street full four inches! Bread, cheese, meat, potatoes,

apples all frozen, where not secured in cellars under ground. At 11, one degree below zero!! (On the 9th and 10th of Decr: when my Thrmr: was down at 0, or zero; & 1 degree below zero—Mr Yalden's Thermr at Newton was at 19, & 22. On Dec: 24, when my Thrmr was at 10½ that at Newton was at 22, & 19. At Newton, when hung side by side, these two instruments accorded exactly.)

Dec. 11.   Grey. Snow. Sun. My apples, pears, & potatoes secured in the cellar, & kitchen-closet; my meat in the cellar. Severe frost, & deep snow. Several men, that were much abroad, made sick by the cold: their hands, & feet were frozen. We hung-out two thermometers, one made by Dollond, & one by B: Martin: the latter was graduated only to 4 below ten, or 6 degrees short of zero: so that when the cold became intense, & our remarks interesting, the mercury went all into the ball, & the instrument was of no service.

Dec. 13.   Strong frost: sun, pleasant. Shoveled out the bostal. Snow very deep still. My laurel-hedge is injured by the cold. Laurus-tines are also hurt.

THE WAKES AND THE TERRACE UNDER SNOW.

'A circumstance that I must not omit, because it was new to us, is, that on *Friday, December* the 10th, being bright sun-shine, the air was full of icy *spiculae*, floating in all directions, like atoms in a sun-beam let into a dark room. We thought them at first particles of the rime falling from my tall hedges; but were soon convinced to the contrary, by making our observations in open places where no rime could reach us.'
(*Selborne*, DB lxiii)

The 'Siberian' conditions continued until the beginning of January 1785. The comparison with Newton Valence interested White, because Newton was 250 feet higher than his own village; he describes what happened as 'this unexpected reverse of comparative local cold'. At Newton the garden trees were unaffected by the frost. At The Wakes the expedient of shaking the snow from the evergreens—to save them from the effects of a second freezing after a temporary thaw—perhaps made matters worse; and the naturalist's walnut tree was so damaged by the cold that it did not bear the following year.

Dec. 14.	Hard frost. Grey & still. Finished shoveling the path to Newton. Dame Loe came to help.
Dec. 15.	Grey & still. Snow drifts on the down, & fills-up the path which we shoveled.

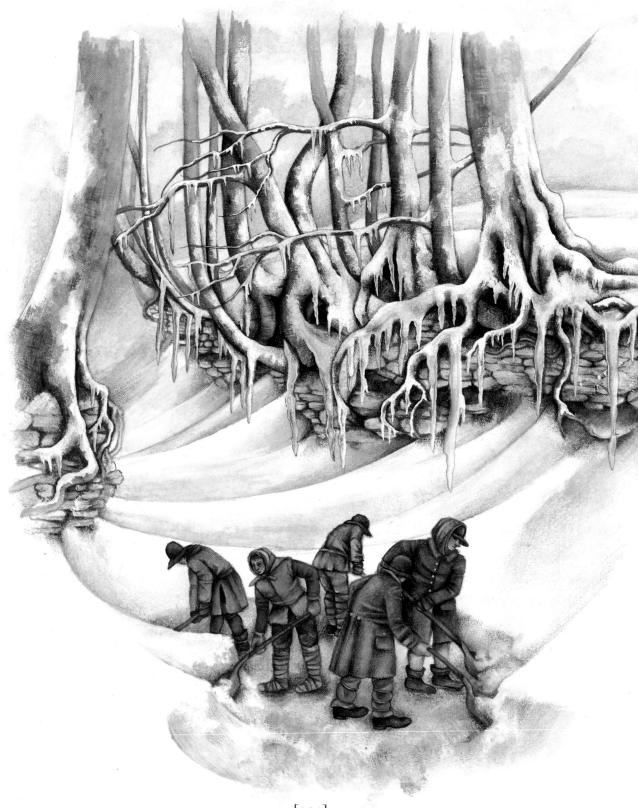

Dec. 16.	Snow, grey. Titmice pull the moss off from trees in searching for insects.
Dec. 17.	Snow in the night. Hard frost, fog, sun. Rime covers the trees. Snow still very deep.

Dec. 20.	Hard frost. Sun. Bright & still.
Dec. 22.	Hard frost. Sun, sharp wind. Farmer Lassom's Dorset-shire ewes begin to lamb. His turnips are frozen as hard as stones.
Dec. 23.	Vast rime. Sun, still. Many labourers were employed in shoveling the snow, & open-ing the hollow, stony lane that leads to the forest. Snow frozen so as almost to bear.
Dec. 24.	Vast rime. Deep fog, still. No wagtails since the snow fell.

HONEY LANE, THE HOLLOW LANE 'LEADING TO THE
FOREST'.
The 'rocky hollow lanes' are in many places 'reduced
sixteen or eighteen feet beneath the level of the fields',
and frostwork can render them fearsome, White says.
(*Selborne*, TP v)

Dec. 25.   Vast rime. Sun, grey. Stagg the keeper, who inhabits the house at the end of Wolmer pond, tells me that he has seen no wild fowl on that lake during the whole frost; & that the entire expanse is entirely frozen-up to such a thickness that the ice would bear a waggon. 500 ducks are seen some times together on that pond.

Dec. 26.   No frost. Sun. Deep, freezing fog.

Dec. 29.   Severe frost. Sun, sharp, sleet.

Dec. 31.   Fog. Grey & still, thaw. Much snow on the ground. My Laurel-hedge, & laurustines quite discoloured, & burnt as it were with the frost.

Rain in Decemr: . . . 3 inch: 6 hund.

Rain at Fyfield in 1784.		Rain at Selborne in 1784.		Rain at S. Lambeth in 1784.	
	inc h		inc h		inc h
Jan:	2: 44	Jan:	3: 18	Jan:	2: 54
Feb:	1: 7	Feb:	0: 77	Feb:	1: 49
March	2: 24	March	3: 82	Mar:	2: 63
April	2: 10	April	3: 92	April	2: 56
May	1: 57	May	1: 52	May	1: 36
June	2: 45	June	3: 65	June	3: 45
July...........	2: 80	July...........	2: 40	July...........	2: 26
Aug:..........	2: 76	August........	3: 88	August........	2: 84
Septr:.........	2: 7	Septr:.........	2: 51	Septr:.........	1: 65
Octr:	0: 17	Octr:	0: 39	Octr:	0: 38
Novr:.........	3: 14	Novr:.........	4: 70	Novr: & }	
Decr:	1: 72	Decr:	3: 6	Decemr: }	5: 60
	24:60		33:80		27:21

Ivy with Berries, *Hedera helix.*